BODY OF EVIDENCE

The Complete

Cases of the Broadway Squad

1940–41

JOHN LAWRENCE

---

illustrations by Peter Kuhlhoff

cover by Rafael deSoto

BLACK MASK

2025

Table of Contents

Body of Evidence

When Michigan Fahey stopped me in that alley and threatened to blast me for sending him up for a five-to-ten I was mad as hell. Then, when I learned the damn fool didn't have any gun, I was just confused—until I saw how the poor stupe had framed himself into a murder rap that even I, his alibi, couldn't break.

THE VOICE, COMING out of the shadows of a high, sandstone stoop, was a strained, harsh undertone "Al. Al Hackett!" I had been looking over the northwest corner of the section as per schedule, and was wandering back towards Broadway across 46th Street. I was in the sullen, cramped and—at one in the morning—dead little block just east of Ninth Avenue. The mouth of an all-night garage three quarters of a block ahead breathed out vague glow but it only thickened the solid blackness along the sagging brownstone fronts near me. I could barely see the man's silhouette hunched beside the stone stairs and, as I stopped abreast of him, the shine of eyes under his peaked cap.

I said, "Well?"

"Remember me, copper?" He was breathing heavily and his voice was a shaky husk. "Remember me? Yeah, you remember me, all right." I realized that his teeth were chattering. He clamped them. "Ted Fahey."

It was maybe a second before I could place him. He was a holdup guy from the midwest, usually known as Michigan Fahey, and I had nailed him peddling some hot bonds in 1934.

Out of curiosity, I tried to see him in the dark. I remembered him as the sheik type, a flashy dresser, Indian-faced except for a pointed nose. He was a gun-toter and none too smart, but he had operated nearly two years in New York before we caught up with him. He wasn't very dressy now. I could see the shine of the safety pin that held his baggy black coat together at the neck and the peaked cap looked far too big for him.

"I thought we settled you for ten," I said.

"Five to ten," he snarled. "I done five—thanks to you and that hypocrite that…" He stopped suddenly, his head jerking round. A clock on a nearby fire-tower bonged somberly—once.

I heard him mutter hastily under his breath, "One o'clock," as he turned back.

He seemed to crouch a little lower and his teeth clenched. "Maybe you remember something I said to you, copper—you and that blabbing rat—in court. I made you both a little promise, due when I got out."

"A promise of what, little man?"

"Of a chunk of lead—right in your great big mouth."

I DIDN'T RECALL it, but I supposed he was stating the truth. No copper with twelve years in quiet clothes can remember all the threats losers sound off with. They average about one for every two convictions and, on Broadway, where every grifter fancies himself as king of the underworld, the percentage is even higher. And unless you're a framer—which I positively am not and never will be—they mean practically nothing. Nine times out of ten, a tough hood going in is just a scared ex-con slinking out. Without friends, money or muscle, there's no more revenge left in them than a rabbit—nine times out of ten. There is, though, the tenth.

"Keep your hands away from your sides," he warned me slatily. "I've got a bead square on your navel. If you want it there, all right."

I was beginning to be able to see him. His hands were sunk deep in his sagging pockets. I didn't recall him as left-handed,

There was a skull and two wax tapers on the desk before him.

which meant that he wasn't, for I wouldn't forget a thing like that. Evidently he planned to shoot me through his right pocket.

I suppose there is something stupider than to stand in pitch darkness, less than three feet from a person and tell that person that you're going to kill him. I can't, however, think what it would be. I let my hands come slowly up, unasked, while I drawled: "So you're going to shoot yourself a cop, eh, you—"

I let him have the toe of my boot—hard—and skipped aside to avoid the shot. There was no shot. He gasped, caught his breath, cramped slowly over, holding himself. He let out a groan that came from his heels. I smashed him upright with a left uppercut that straightened him into the full force of my right poke to the side of his chin. He was knocked kicking down the little areaway's one step.

His head *thwocked* on the cement floor and he skidded, doubled up, against the stone wall of the house and lay still. He was out cold, groaning and twitching like a dreaming dog when I splashed light from my flash and knelt down to fumble for his gun.

But he had no gun.

It took me about four minutes to confirm that bewildering fact—to search his shabby, second-hand coat and prison suit, to scout all around the nearby ground, and to realize he hadn't so much as a toothpick on him.

I smelled his breath. He had been drinking, all right but I couldn't tell if he were really drunk—although reason told me he must be, to pull a stunt like this.

I felt like hell. All right, he had been a gun-toter and he might be dangerous again, but he was a down-and-outer now and I had twenty pounds and three inches on him. I felt like a louse for giving him such severe business, although I was damned if I could see what else he could expect under the circumstances. He was damned lucky I hadn't blasted his face off.

I had really taken him seriously. He must have gone a little stir-simple and, on the strength of a couple of drinks, had himself a brainstorm.

I stood first on one foot, then the other, looking down at him, not just knowing what to do. I couldn't run him in, even if I hadn't felt that he'd had enough. The Marquis—Lieutenant Marquis, my boss on the Broadway Squad—would crucify me.

We—the Squad—were supposed to be little tin gods on

wheels. The idea of locking up a down-at-heels, unarmed, penniless stir-bug because he threatened one of us would bring a great belly-laugh from the clowns down at headquarters.

I tried to find out if he were badly hurt. His pulse was strong and regular and his breathing, though a little gasping, sounded all right.

I didn't think he needed any hospitalization.

It looked like the only thing to do was just leave him here. To wake up alone where he was would give him the proper idea of his own importance and furthermore, in case he started another brainstorm, as he well might, I would not be around where he could start a ruckus and possibly force me to take him in.

IT SEEMED A little unusual to walk off and leave him unconscious, but I couldn't see anything better to do. There seemed no point in making trouble for the goof. If this was the best he could do, I wasn't much worried from now on. I found his hat and put it on his head and went on about my business.

I did tell a prowl-car sergeant that I'd seen a drunk lying in that areaway, just to make sure he didn't up and croak or something. The prowler drove by the spot about half an hour later. Fahey was gone by then.

He hung around in my mind, however—partly because my rounds were dull and I had nothing else to think about, and partly because my memory wouldn't cog. I couldn't dredge up the details of the job we'd hung on him, nor the name of the squealer—or complainant—against whom the ex-con also evidently thought he had a grudge. I had it in mind—if I could think of the bird's name—to give him a friendly call. Not that

I had the slightest worry about Fahey's deadliness now, but a lug like that can be an awful nuisance.

I knew damned well I should have the name—this complainant's—at my fingertips, but it eluded me till I made my regular two-o'clock stop at the Times Square Ticket Agency—the unofficial headquarters of the Broadway Squad—and asked around.

Not that he was any nationally famous figure or anything like that, but we were all interested in him because he was a Broadway sharpshooter who had got religion. Really got it, I mean, not just adopted it with an angle in mind. Maybe I shouldn't call him a sharpshooter, but he was barely a hairline the other side of it at one time. His name was Harry Nirdlinger and he had once been a 'private handicapper' for a bunch of stockbrokers, till too many of his horses dropped dead at the post. Then he went out west and got into the racetrack wire-service and really built himself up to something. Unfortunately, the big syndicate came along and invited him to hand it over to them. He tried to buck them and in less than a year they had him in involuntary bankruptcy.

Even that didn't lick him. He struggled out of it somehow and squared off again. But he'd been married in the meantime and he finally made peace. The syndicate bought him out and offered him the job of district manager for them in New York. It was while he was here looking the situation over that Michigan Fahey stuck him up on his way from a safety-deposit box to his hotel and lifted eighteen thousand dollars' worth of sugar bonds, which I ultimately caught him trying to fence. We recovered all but one bond, as I recalled it.

Nirdlinger finally took the syndicate job and settled in New

York, but after a year he suddenly joined this very strict sect called the Gospel Brothers, threw up his job and, from what I heard, gave most of his dough to the Brothers' treasury. He was currently around Broadway, not doing anything, but willing at the drop of a hat to struggle for hours to proselyte anyone who would listen. He was especially down on horse-racing and, as far as I had heard, hadn't scored any converts yet. If this makes him sound like a gaunt-eyed fanatic, then it sounds wrong. He was tall, slender, electrically handsome, even in his middle forties, with wavy brown hair and sparkling black eyes, one of which had a very slight cast in it, which served only to make him look merrier. He did have a fanatic's harsh mouth, however.

I dug out the carbon copy of my last report on the five-year-old case and found that he had lived then at the Brunswick. I gave the hotel a call and found that he was registered there, but not in at the moment. It was just off Broadway on 54th Street, and on my regular route, so I tucked the report in my pocket and continued on my beat, with intent to drop in there later.

HE STILL WASN'T in, after half an hour, according to Wheeler, the pop-eyed night clerk. The Brunswick was a seedy, mahogany-panelled ancient little fleabag, half full of hustlers, half of ancient, tarnished celebrities. The lobby was a dim little gloomy foyer, with dark settees here and there behind potted palms. Wheeler leaned his elbows on the desk and inspected his polished fingernails.

"Yeah, he's usually in at this time," he said in answer to my question. "He can't have gone far, because his key's not in the rack." I didn't see the need of the softness of his voice till he made a slight head motion and added: "There's another one waiting for him—his wife."

"Where?" I said, after a casual look.

He let his eyes roll around, then leaned across the desk to peer at a palm-shadowed club chair. "Oops, sorry. I guess she got tired waiting and left."

I said, "Yeah," and looked at the open mouth of the dark mahogany stairs a few yards from where he indicated she had been sitting. "Wait a minute. Doesn't she live with him?"

"Hell, no—not for the last two years. They're divorced."

I mused on that and straggled as far as the door, before it occurred to me to write Nirdlinger a note. I took out my notebook and scribbled on a page, with the idea of leaving it in his box. But the elevators in the Brunswick are much closer to the door than the desk—one of the reasons the hustlers like the place—and the uniformed boy in the open car was, for a miracle, awake. I stepped in and rode to the third floor—I already knew Nirdlinger's room number.

However, I had to plot out my way among the dingy corridors on the third floor—the Brunswick is much larger than it looks from its postage-stamp lobby—and it was while I was groping my way toward 318 that I passed young Murray Dietz.

He didn't know me, but I knew him all right. He was a good-looking, husky blond youth who still looked like a college boy. He came down the corridor a little unsteadily, his hat pulled low on his curly golden hair, his pale-blue, bright eyes a little bloodshot and two spots of high fever in the blond face he tried to hide from me in the turned-up collar of his tweed coat.

I was a little surprised to see him in here, but in a hotel full of charmers, you're likely to see anybody. Even multi-millionaire's nephews. I wondered how his tight-fisted, Baptist uncle would regard the matter. The old pirate, after a lifetime of fast dealing in the coal business had decided or, as I heard it, been talked into, building a vast office building near to Radio Center, as a sort of memorial. The youngster, Murray—I guess he was a good piece over thirty, at that—had, presumably, done the talking into and was in charge of the whole project. If I were laying out millions I don't think I'd care to have *my* straw-boss cavorting about the Brunswick, but what the hell? It wasn't my business—definitely. If we tried to interest ourselves in all the angles we get on the great and near-great, in Broadway's back doors, we'd go crazy.

I finally found 318 and stooped to slide my note under the door. It went easily enough—the doors don't fit any too well in the Brunswick. I gave it a final poke with my finger so no lingering corner would stick out, straightened up and walked away.

I was halfway back to the elevator when I noticed my finger.

I stopped as though I'd run into a wall.

I ran back, grabbed the knob—and the door opened inwards. I snatched for the light switch just inside the room and let the door close behind me.

The first thing I saw was the huge, irregular splotch of dark on the taupe carpet. Broken glass glittered redly where it lay on the discoloration.

A bald-headed man sat with his back to me in a robe of white wool, cowled like a monk's robe. That is, it had been white. It was streaked and stained with bright red now, even where it could be seen from the back. He sat at the writing-desk, which had been moved out into the center of the room and his bald head lay on one shoulder.

Two long strides took me around to where I could see his face. It was Nirdlinger's face. This was the first time anybody on Broadway knew he wore a toupée. His arms were crossed on the desk in front of him and his head lolled. It lolled because it was scarcely connected to his body any longer. His throat was a raw crimson gash, yawning open. Blood had gushed and poured down his white robe, drenched his bare feet and knees. There was a book, completely soaked in blood, open on the desk before him, and between his crossed arms was a papier-mâché skull. Two wax tapers were in holders at either end of the little desk. The telephone stood on its head drunkenly, propped against the wall, standing, by a freak of fate so that its hook was depressed. On the floor between table and telephone lay the jagged, smashed-off neck of a quart bottle. The vicious, sawtooth edges of the thing were bloodstained, but not the actual neck-top. Nirdlinger's black eyes, with their slight cast, shone at me merrily as though he were relishing some monstrous joke.

And I—I had dismissed Michigan Fahey as harmless.

That was the first thing that poked a galvanizing finger through the shock of finding the ex-tout-fanatic dead. I had casually tagged the ex-convict as no more than a possible nuisance, let him rove around free, even after he had pulled his crazy play with me! What a squeeze I was in, if *that* ever got out.

I TURNED TOWARD the telephone—and then thought of fingerprints. I saw the fibre-tagged key of the room lying on the untouched bed and grabbed it up as I strode for the door. I didn't know of any telephone nearer than the lobby so

I hurried down the hall and dropped down the stairs. Fortunately, there were pay booths in the lobby—not just lines to the switchboard—and I got the Ticket Agency without having to fear being listened in on. Big Johnny Berthold answered and I gave him a rough sketch of what had happened. The Marquis happened to be in the Agency and Big Johnny relayed the news to him, and he, unaware of how I was tied into it, saw no reason why I shouldn't notify the Homicide Squad at once.

I did that, and then sat in the booth, flaying my brain as to where I might be able to find the swarthy little maniac. I had to start from scratch and I had to consider how things looked, but I saw no reason why I shouldn't put out a radio alarm so I did that. As soon as I had, I regretted it. If somebody else collared the ex-convict before I did....

I tried the Parole Board's night man, but that was stupid. Fahey wasn't on parole.

I tried one or two people in the Bowery that might give me a tip, but they had no news of him.

I finally thought of the carbon copy of my report on the five-year-old holdup and got it out of my pocket. It showed that Fahey had lived at the time of his arrest on West 54th Street, little more than a block from night court. I recognized the address. It was a thieves kitchen if ever there was one—a small, dingy apartment house that no honest man had ever been known to enter.

It was, of course, a crazy long shot that he would be living there again, but people seem to do that in New York and anyway it was the only one in my locker. Furthermore, the joint was only a few steps away and I could take a crack at it and be back almost as soon as Homicide arrived.

I threw the key on the desk as I hurried out and almost turned Wheeler's hair white by telling him I had locked the door and it wasn't to be unlocked till the headquarters boys arrived.

A CAB TOOK me across 54th. The joint was a five-story building that had once been white stone. Two dim carriage lamps shone at either side of the entrance. There was no one in the smelly lobby and no sign of name bells or who lived there. I rode the self-service elevator to the fourth floor and walked softly to Apartment E—the one-room scatter he had had before. Nothing of the silence, dimness or stink of the building had changed in five years.

I drew a blank, of course. The apartment—the scissored-out center of a business card tacked to the door told me—was occupied now by Paul Muhl. I knew him—a wizened little shyster who, by all rights, should have been gathered in with Nick Fontana's vice mob, but who had somehow got over-looked. I took a peek through the old-fashioned keyhole—despite the snappy lock higher up, it was still unblocked—and saw him in socks and shirt-sleeves, reading a racing-form.

I knocked and he opened up, stuck his slack-mouthed red face and half-bald, corrugated head around the edge of the door. The lids of his green eyes made straight lines across the eyeballs, giving him a dopey, dull look. He grunted glumly. "Oh, you, sergeant."

"Yeah. I'm looking for Michigan Fahey."

He blinked curiously. "So?"

"You wouldn't know where he is?"

He blinked again. "What is this? I just barely heard of the

guy. Why would I…?"

"He hasn't been around here? This is his old apartment."

"It is? Hell no, I haven't seen him."

I left him looking around the one room with new interest and went back down—and almost ran into the girl.

She was trying to get into the elevator as I got off—evidently thinking it was her own button-pushing that had brought it down, not mine.

We stopped, inches apart, on the open threshold of the car.

I started to make a wise-crack—and didn't.

She wasn't the type. She wasn't, come to think of it—and this is why I took notice of her—the type to be within a million miles of a drum like this. Her eyes were fiery brown stars, her uncovered head a mass of smoothly waving mahogany glow. She was under medium height, but the proud tilt of her chin and the carriage of her little hour-glass figure seemed to make her taller. Her skin was like milk, her features small, delicate. Her white ermine evening wrap was open, showing the green-and-gold bodice above her long black velvet skirt. Her hands and feet were tiny and graceful, and she was so imperious that I automatically obeyed the impatient little gesture of her green glove and scurried out of her way, mumbling apologies.

Wondering what in the world she was doing here almost stopped me but the pressure of the business in hand nudged me and I went back to the Brunswick.

COPPERS, PHOTOGRAPHERS, FINGERPRINT men, M.E.'s men, crammed the death room, spilling out in the hall which was besieged by reporters. They had sprung up out of the ground and there was talk, talk, talk.

I spotted the Marquis, dapper in his black clothes, his pink-cheeked round face blank while his somber blue eyes missed nothing. Big Johnny Berthold stood in a corner with him, his too-small hat on the back of his shaggy blond mane, his hands behind him in unconscious imitation of the Marquis' pose.

I was jumped by the Homicide Squad but I told them my piece in about three minutes. Men were coming and going, reporting to the skeleton-faced, green-eyed Lieutenant Lebaron whose painfully thin, carefully dressed figure stood in the middle of the room directing all this. I eased over beside the Marquis and we exchanged nods. The doctor from the M.E.'s office was packing up his kit.

A prowl-car cop suddenly appeared at the door, waving a large square blue card—a rogue's gallery file-card. He had trouble getting in and called: "Lieutenant—hey, Lieutenant—here's Michigan Fahey's fingerprints you phoned for...."

Lebaron snatched them and barked "Murphy!" at a man huddled over a portable fingerprint outfit on the bed. He handed him the card over the ducking head of a detective, and I slid over in time to see the broken bottle-neck lying on a clean towel on the bed, dusted with white powder.

A second later, I heard the fingerprint man say: "Yep. They're his, all right. Fahey's."

Up till there, everything went grimly according to Hoyle.

Then it turned abruptly haywire.

There just happened to be enough quiet in the room for me to hear the M.E.'s doctor say: "Yes, I agree with your time of death perfectly. He was evidently phoning and didn't hear the door open behind him. The killer knocked him unconscious with a blow of that bottle, breaking it, then cut him to pieces with the jagged end. The phone was undoubtedly knocked out of his hand by the blow and lit as it is, causing the switchboard to think Nirdlinger had hung up."

I asked one of the detectives idly: "What time was he killed?"

"Right on the dot of one o'clock."

"*What?*"

"Yeah. Some dame was talking to him—called him up, and was cut off right then, the switchboard guy says, and a bird across the hall heard a crash just about then in here."

I managed to hold my tongue, but it was with an effort.

One o'clock! At one o'clock I had been messing about with Michigan Fahey on West Forty-sixth Street. I distinctly remembered the fire-tower clock striking the hour!

For just a second I wondered giddily if the seemingly simple ex-con were running some Machiavellian scheme here—if he had somehow managed to make it *appear* that Nirdlinger had been killed at one o'clock, knowing that I would come to the front for him and….

I couldn't swallow it. I couldn't see that much cleverness in the Indian-faced ex-heister. Neither could I make myself believe the M.E.'s office could make such a mistake. And the momentary question only re-doubled my realization of the clear, cold, fact. Michigan Fahey had not killed the ex-tout-fanatic!

I HASTILY SIGNALED to the Marquis and Big Johnny, led them out, casually, till we got far enough around corridors to be out of sight. "Fahey didn't kill this guy," I told them quickly. "It's a frame—fingerprints or no fingerprints."

"How do you know?"

I told them: "He was on Forty-sixth Street, waiting for me. He popped out at me, just as one o'clock was striking as a matter of fact. He was talking wild—threatening to shoot me. Only he didn't have a gun. Of course, I didn't know that till after I laid him out. I left him in an areaway over there. As a matter of fact, I sent Symonds, in a prowl car over there about half an hour later to see if—that is, I told Symonds I'd seen a lush there...." I trailed off.

It did sound awfully ragged. If I hadn't realized it for myself, the queer stares that had grown in both their eyes while I got it out would have told me.

The Marquis' soft voice said: "Wait now, Hack. Let's tell it again."

I told it again, while I felt color rise in my face.

The Marquis catalogued: "You were on Forty-sixth. Nobody else was anywhere near. Michigan jumps out of an areaway, announces he's going to shoot you. What with? His finger?"

"It was pitch dark. I thought he had a gun in his pocket."

"So a clock rings out one o'clock and you kick him into an areaway, knock him cold, and walk off whistling. My God, Hack!"

My face burned. "It wasn't exactly as dumb as that. It was too dark to see and he braced me, didn't he? He stepped out as though he *had* a gun and—well, I gave him the foot. He didn't seem to be worth running in. I—uh—just sent Symonds around to make sure he wasn't seriously hurt or anything. I knew you wouldn't want a punk like that to think he was worth our time."

The Marquis' face was concerned. "You insist it was one o'clock?"

"Sure. When the clock struck, he even mentioned..." I wished I hadn't brought that up.

The Marquis' head cocked to one side. "What'd you do? Have a chummy little chat? Mister do you realize how this is going to sound when the newspaper wits start on it? You're going to think you've stepped in flypaper."

"I can't help that."

He looked at the floor thoughtfully, shook his head almost absently. "Well, suppose we all go and have a talk with him, Hack," he suggested.

I felt the vein pound in my forehead. "—— you! I don't know where he is. And I'm not faking an alibi for him either. You've got so damn many takers on your squad that you think everybody is on the make. I'm not—and if I were, I wouldn't start by covering up a killing for a no-account slob like that."

He scanned my eyes, then nodded. "You've got something there, son. I guess the best thing is just to skip it, eh?"

"What? And let him take a framed rap?"

"Oh, I dare say the downtown boys will get at the truth, sooner or later."

"In a pig's eye! I'm his only out, and you know it! And I don't go for frames, chief. We've had that out before. I don't care if every rag in town laugh themselves sick at the story—that poor dope has an alibi and somebody else killed Nirdlinger and is trying to frame Fahey."

The Marquis' eyes came up quickly. "Somebody else? You mean you have a line...?"

"Maybe I have," I raged. "That's not the point."

"Be reasonable, Hack," his quiet voice cut across mine. "Before you make a mess, why not scout around and see if you can get a line on the real killer. Then maybe you can spring this—alibi. Or maybe you won't need to."

"So you ——s think I'm lying."

"No. No. But alibiing an ex-convict murderer doesn't look good, under any conditions. With a story that will be as vulnerable as that in print—or in court—against fingerprint evidence—well, if somebody else did do it, why not locate him? You've got the inside track."

I was good and mad. "If you think I won't, you're crazy," I snapped at them and left them standing there.

I STRODE BACK to the elevator and rode down, dug Wheeler out of a mob of reporters and took him back to the manager's office. "If you know where Mrs. Nirdlinger lives, tell me and nobody else," I told him.

He didn't know where she lived but he did know her phone number, having called it for Nirdlinger. I checked with downtown and found it was an extremely modest, quiet little hotel on West 79th.

Somehow, there was enough surprise in it when I phoned the hotel and found that she was still out, to send me grimly scooting up there in a cab.

It was a spare, neat, clean little place, something like a rooming-house in that it had no bellboy service and a lobby the size of a good-sized bathroom. The plump little man in gray behind the miniature desk-and-switchboard was smoking a cigar and he got very concerned over my inquiries.

He said, "Yah?" astoundedly when I told him that Mrs. Nirdlinger's husband had been killed. He assured me that she had not come in since my call, but that she would surely be along any minute. He had 'accidentally' overheard her talking to friends whom she was meeting at the Club Vincennes at a little after one o'clock. She often did this—went out to night clubs alone.

He parked me in one of the two club chairs that the little lobby boasted, and I waited.

She came in—and then I did get a surprise. Light glinted on her mahogany curls and her chin was just as imperiously up as when I had run into her down in that dingy thieves' kitchen on 54th. Her white ermine wrap was drawn tight around her now and that was the only difference.

I was so startled that I sat just where I was, despite the eyebrow waving of the plump night clerk, and let him ferry her up out of sight on the single cage-elevator. Then I, in turn, rode up with him and, following his whispered directions, turned and walked straight to the back of the little sixth-floor corridor.

She had her door open, was wiggling to get the jammed key out of the lock when she noticed me, gave me a sharp, censorious look from her shining brown eyes—and then went motionless as she, presumably, recognized me. She frowned.

I said: "Mrs. Nirdlinger, may I come in a moment? I have some serious news for you."

"Really?" There was disinterested sharpness in her tone. "I'm afraid I shouldn't be interested at this time of night. Please...."

I showed her my palmed badge.

It brought a little annoyed frown to her forehead and made the sparkle in her brown eyes a little darker.

"I—uh—saw you earlier in the evening," I said.

"I know you did," she answered. "What has that to do with this?"

"It's hardly a matter to be discussed in a hall."

She finally shrugged. "Oh, all right." She led me into a minia-ture two-room-and-bath suite, and I took off my hat. She faced me from a mantel, pulling off her gloves. "Now, suppose you tell me your business, Mr. Officer. I hope it's legitimate, for I am not accustomed…."

"That building on Fifty-fourth you went into," I said. "It's well known to the police as a hang-out for crooks. Whomever you went to see there, we would doubt that your business there was legitimate."

Her eyes blazed. "Would you indeed? Well, permit me to tell you…"

"Whom did you go to see?" I was getting a little sharper with her.

HER LIPS TIGHTENED. "It is no business of yours whatever. As it happens, I am—" She broke off, thinking care-fully. "I guess there's no harm in telling you. I am having a little litigation and I went there to see a person about it."

"What litigation, Mrs. Nirdlinger? I can find that out by a look at court records, you know."

She drew herself up. "I am suing Dietz Center, for negli-gence. I was hit by a falling stone, in my back, while passing there. It may put an end to my career as a dancer."

I groped. "And you were at that building looking for—what? A witness?"

"I—yes, a witness. I—the person I was seeking doesn't seem to be in at regular hours and so I…."

"What is the name of this witness?" She drew herself up. "I am sure that is no concern of yours."

I was, of course, groping dizzily when I asked: His name wouldn't be Fahey, by any chance?"

She stared at me stonily. "No."

I started another tack. "Did you happen to drop in to see your husband, while you were down there?"

Her eyes did not change their stoniness. "I attempted to. I had been talking to him earlier and he hung up. I went over there, but he had gone out."

"Do you mind telling me what it was that you had to see him about?"

"He had called and left word that he wanted to see me, before I phoned him. We had barely gotten started talking when he... How dare you? What possible right have you to ask such questions?"

"Believe me, Mrs. Nirdlinger, you will be answering more questions than mine, almost immediately. I am terribly sorry to tell you, but your husband was killed tonight."

For a second, it did not seem to register. She stared at me, while the color slowly went out of her face. She finally gulped: "Dead? Killed? Harry—dead?"

Two great tears squeezed themselves out from under her lashes. She choked, "Oh, excuse me," and stumbled into the bathroom.

When she came out a minute later, her eyes were wild, her face like chalk under her rouge, but she was dry-eyed. She drove at me in a voice so husky as to be almost inaudible: "How? What happened? Where is he? Take me to...."

"You won't be allowed to see him till tomorrow," I soothed her. "Please just take it easy, Mrs. Nirdlinger. There are certain formalities to be observed in a case like this. Since you were in the vicinity of his hotel tonight, we will have to get a statement from you. Suppose I get the clerk up—I noticed he was a notary—and you can give me a complete statement of everything you did tonight. Then you can sign it and I guarantee you will have a minimum of trouble from now on."

Her eyes were vacant, squeezed with grief. "Yes, yes," and then, as I started for the phone, she cried sharply, almost sobbingly, "Oh, no, no. I can't sign anything. I forgot. This—this litigation—I have given my complete power of attorney to my representative and promised not to sign...."

"That won't interfere with this," I assured her. "If you prefer not to sign it, the witnessed statement will be just as good." I called up the clerk.

I asked her gently, "You were still fond of your husband?"

SHE WAS A dazed, frantic girl now, the imperiousness temporarily driven right out of her. She said desperately: "Yes, yes, God help me. I—there's no reason why I should be. He's—I guess he never loved me, but I—that's why I went to see him tonight."

"What?" I said quickly. "Why did you go to see him tonight?"

"To tell him he couldn't interfere—that even I couldn't stop the lawsuit now—to tell him I'd signed everything over."

"He was against the lawsuit?"

"He—I thought he would be, if he heard of it. And when he called me—I thought he'd heard of it—thought that was why he wanted to see me."

"How would he be able to stop it?" I asked bewilderedly. "You're divorced. He has no claim on you."

There was a queer sob in her throat. It made no impression on her face. She nursed one wrist and stared at the rug with torn eyes. "He—he could make me do anything he wanted," she blurted desperately. "He—I never could refuse him anything. When he was in trouble—even before we were married—he took everything I owned—the little theater my first husband left me. That's how he got out of his trouble."

"He didn't pay you for it?"

"Oh he paid me ten thousand dollars, but I know he sold it for more—much more," she said wildly. "And then when he—he went crazy over this Gospel Brothers thing, they—they told him he shouldn't have a wife. That—that was why we were divorced...."

She buried her head in her hands and burst into sobs.

There was a tap on the door. I went over, expecting the night clerk from below. Lebaron and a beefy detective of his Homicide Squad named Stark were outside the door. The skeleton-faced Homicide lieutenant bowed over his hat and said, before he realized: "Good-evening, Mrs. Nirdlinger. We've been trying to get you all eve..." He compressed his lips as he saw me and said dully: "Oh. Hello, Hackett. What are you after here?"

There was no use my trying to get any further with him around so I said: "I was going to take a statement from Mrs. Nirdlinger, but you can do it as well. Thank you very much, Mrs. Nirdlinger."

Before the muddiness in Lebaron's eyes cleared, I was out and past them.

On the street in front of the little building, I saw the prowl car that had brought them up. Smitty, not a bad guy for a Homicide dick, was alone at the wheel. I slanted over and asked him: "What brought Lebaron up here?" Smitty stopped humming long enough to shrug and say: "I dunno. He got to worrying when he couldn't get hold of her by phone. Thought maybe Fahey had decided to polish her off, too."

I WAS TEMPTED to force my way in to see young Murray Dietz, even at this hour, but I didn't have the heart. Instead, I did some intense thinking, plus a lot of worrying, snatched a few hours sleep and started after him in the morning.

He had an office high up in Radio City, where he could watch the skeleton of his own building slowly rising, a short piece north. I started dropping in on him at twelve but it was nearly three before I got word that he was in and was asked to wait in the chromium-and-blue office. Meanwhile, I had read the papers.

They gave the murder a terrific play, and they had the ex-convict Fahey all but electrocuted. He was painted as a dangerous homicidal maniac. Police, said the original phrase, were combing the city for him.

I was ushered into a spacious, bright room on the west side of the building, with a vast window overlooking Sixth Avenue. Murray Dietz was standing, looking out the window, his hands clasped behind him. When he turned to look at me, his face was exactly as it had been last night in the Brunswick corridor—spotted with fever. There was no recognition in his blood-streaked eyes. I guess he had been too busy trying to avoid being tagged himself to take any notice of me the last time I had seen him.

I showed him my badge and said: "I saw you last night, Mr. Dietz, just outside the door of this Nirdlinger that was killed."

His red-streaked blue eyes looked at me stonily. "I'm afraid you're mistaken, Mr. Detective. I wasn't in any Brunswick Hotel last night."

That changed everything. All of a sudden, I felt as though I had ground under my feet. I said slowly: "It's too bad I saw you." I tried to put together enough fragments of what I had learned to at least scare him. "There's a story going round that you went to see Nirdlinger because his ex-wife was suing you. You knew he had great influence with her and you wanted the suit called off. He refused and you—in a moment of drunken fury—gave him the business."

It was a total flop. He said stonily: "Except that I wasn't in the Brunswick last night, and that we have already approved settlement of Mrs. Nirdlinger's just claim, that story is splendid."

I had a flash of pure genius, although I was more than half guessing. I stepped over and looked up the street to the rising, two square blocks of steel-and-mortar that was—or would be—Dietz Center. I said musingly: "Funny how your affairs keep running into the Nirdlinger's. They used to own a little theater—somewhere along there, right about where your building will stand."

He shrugged.

I said: "So you weren't at the Brunswick—any time between twelve thirty and two thirty, eh?"

His jaws were tight. He stepped over and touched a button on the desk. After a second, a stocky, gray-haired man with the build of a wrestler and grim, grape-blue eyes came in. He looked as though he hoped I would start something and, in spite of his toupée-like shining little dab of black hair, I don't know but what he could have taken me.

"This gentleman wants to know where I was last night," Dietz said, "between twelve thirty and two thirty, Webster."

"Why," the other said, "you was with Counsellor Penhorwood and me, in the counsellor's apartment on Park."

We looked at each other for two or three minutes. "I think I can break that," I told them finally. "If I do, you'll all three stew."

It didn't seem to worry them. I was the one who flushed. "All right," I promised. "I'll see you again, Mr. Dietz."

I HAD SOME routine work to do that kept me a little while—not intense enough to stop my worrying about the wretched ex-con, however—and I didn't finish it till dinner time. I ate and went over to the Agency.

Somebody said, "There he is now," and someone else shouted: "Wait a minute. Hold the line. He just came in." I went over and the group around a desk broke apart to let me pick up the phone. "Hello... Yeah, Hackett."

A husky voice—I couldn't mistake it, I swear—snarled in my ear: "I got a gun now, you ———. You're next—and then that lousy skirt that squealed on me." The whack of the receiver nearly took my eardrum off.

"Who was it?" Big Johnny asked when we'd had no success tracing the call.

"Michigan Fahey," I said. "Want to make something of it?"

I jammed my hands in my pockets and went out. Half a block up Broadway, the Marquis was sitting alone in McGuire's big red convertible, listening to the police radio calls. He called me over.

"Well?" he said, when I had told him about the call. "Does

that make any difference to your—uh—frame-feelings?"

"Not a damned bit," I said. "He was saying what he was told—" I broke off as I got the drift of the radio broadcast.

"… repeat on order #367. Regarding Theodore Fahey, alias Michigan Fahey, five feet six, dark hair, dark skin, pointed nose, dark eyes, last seen wearing peaked cap and… etc. This man is dangerous, wanted for murder. Officers will be prepared to shoot on sight."

"That's a —— —— shame!" I blurted.

"Why don't you just skip it, Hack?" his soft voice suggested. "You can get yourself in a dirty mess."

"I don't believe in frames!" I told him.

I went on up the street and parked in a dark doorway, trying to think. I didn't quite get the allusion to a 'skirt that squealed on me.'

Then I felt quickly and found I was still carrying around the carbon copy of the report on the five-year-old holdup. I got it out and discovered that the alarm—five years ago—had first been turned in by Mrs. Nirdlinger, while her husband was still unconscious from a crack on the head.

Light dawned.

I guess I wasted two or three minutes with my jaw sagging, before I turned and went into a cigar store—a couple more with my hand on the receiver, before I called Mrs. Nirdlinger.

"You must listen very carefully to what I say and do exactly what I tell you," I impressed on her. "Will you trust me—for tonight only?"

"Oh, yes, yes," she said frightenedly. "What…?"

"Call Mr. Murray Dietz and tell him you must see him tonight and that it will be to his advantage."

"But—but I don't know him!"

"No matter. I think he'll be glad to come."

"But what—if he does come, what will I say—I don't understand…."

"I think he will make all the conversation necessary. Just tell him to bring along any papers he has around."

She gasped. "Papers!"

"Yeah. Legal papers. Are there any detectives hanging around your place now? Did Lebaron leave anyone?"

"Yes, two men. I—I don't know just where they are…."

"Do you know their names?"

"Yes. A Mr. Sparks and a Mr. Haberman…."

"That's fine," I outranked both of them. "And under no conditions tell anybody who it was that suggested this to you. Understand? No one must know I had anything to do with it."

"But—but what are—what is going to happen?"

"That's up to you. By signing a paper or two, you may be able to clear this whole situation up, get yourself clear of any danger…."

"But I can't sign papers! I'll get into trouble if I do!"

"You'll get into worse if you don't," I said and hung up.

I hung around a corner soft-drink stand and drank a couple of pineapple drinks, then called her back. "Did you get hold of him?"

"Oh, yes, yes, but—"

"When's he coming?"

"N-nine o'clock. Are you…?"

"I'll give you a ring around then. Or be there."

I MADE A mistake, of course, in not going up there earlier

than I did. I dropped off my cab on Columbus, just below 79th Street, strolled round the corner and got into a building-front opposite her hotel, just at eight thirty.

It was a quiet street. Cars went through it but none stopped near enough to me to attract my attention, till five minutes to nine. I almost missed the one that did, at that. I had my eye on the building adjoining Mrs. Nirdlinger's. It was some two stories lower than hers and, if my geography didn't trick me, its roof would be about level with her windows—or some of them, at any rate.

Sharp at five to nine, a taxi stopped across the street from me and let out the husky, hurrying figure of young Murray Dietz, carrying a briefcase. He stopped a minute, peering up at the building, then went inside. I could see him querying the desk clerk, then board the elevator.

I took one last look up and down the street, a little put out, if the truth must be known, and then followed him inside.

I caught the cage elevator as it came down from taking him up and rode to her floor where I caught sight of Sparks, the headquarters dick, in a shadowy corner and beckoned him over.

"Go down and take a plant in the doorway of the building next door. What kind of a joint is it?"

"It's an empty rooming-house. They're going to tear it down. Haberman is already planted in the front door...."

"Then you go to the back and stay around there."

I gave him no chance to argue, went on down the hall. I didn't want to let the conversation in that little suite go unguided too long.

She opened promptly when I knocked. She had on a royal-blue house coat and bright red slippers and she was a tasty dish.

I could see Dietz' hard hat and gloves on the mantel beyond her. Her eyes looked at me wildly and she whispered: "He's— he's here...."

"I know." I walked ahead of her along the little foyer into the living-room.

One quick glance gave me the setup. The two-rooms-and-bath suite was really one large room with a bathroom plumped down in the middle of it, against the side wall. The bathroom door was open a couple of feet into the living-room and though it was dark inside, I could see the curtains stirring faintly on the raised window.

Dietz' face was like granite and his eyes blazed. "You, eh, Mr. Detective? Am I to assume that this arrangement...?"

"Relax," I told him. "We are gathered here together—well, we aim to clear up a couple of points." I took a quick step through the archway into the tiny bedroom, asking, "There isn't anyone in here, is there?" but there wasn't.

Color began to come and go in Dietz' face. The girl was huddled motionless against the mantel, her hands clasped in front of her, watching me with a sort of fascination. I estimated carefully, went over and stood beside a wing chair—about the only spot in the room directly in line with both the open bathroom door and the open bathroom window. I held my hat in my hands.

"You"—I nodded at the girl—"transferred your Alhambra Theater some ten years ago, to your husband, while he was having his trouble. Right?"

"Y-yes," she breathed.

"He, in turn, sold it to"—I nodded at Dietz—"you. The same day, or practically the same day."

I PROCEEDED. "TIME marches on. Presently the Dietz Center has accumulated all the parcels of land in those two blocks so they announce their plans and get going on their building. You," I told Dietz, "originated the whole idea, talked your uncle into it, and into giving you the job of putting it up. I guess you thought you were putting yourself into a soft job, but from what I hear of construction these days, it's a head-ache—even to an experienced man. I imagine you probably had more than your share of troubles all along, but nothing like this last one, eh?"

I looked over at the girl. "You said you gave absolute power of attorney to your lawyer. When did you do it?"

"Just—just about two weeks ago."

"All right." I turned back to Dietz. "So three weeks ago, Mrs. Nirdlinger gave you the sad news, eh?"

"Four," he said hoarsely.

I had to ponder that for a second. "I get it," I said. "The damage suit was a cover-up. You knew you were stuck on the other and that you had to pay. But your uncle, eh? You were afraid if he found out what a damned fool you'd made of your-self on the go-in, he'd clamp down on you—maybe even toss you right out on your ear. So you conceived the idea of the damage suit, so that you could pay off—how much?"

"A hundred and fifty thousand dollars."

I whistled softly. "A nice sum. You can buy a lot of murder with that."

The girl cried out desperately: "What are you talking about? I don't understand! A stone did fall on me…."

"Sure, sure," I soothed her. "But don't go *too* virtuous on us, Mrs. Nirdlinger. I shouldn't wonder if—assuming a brick did fall on you—it was all nicely cooked up long before you went near the construction. But don't get excited. I'm not going to make any trouble about that. Except that it helps explain your husband's death."

"My hus— Oh my God, how?"

"He was killed because he would have kicked over the little deal that meant a fortune for his murderer. You said yourself that he could make you do anything. Well, he would have made you turn thumbs down on this racket—although I think you would have done that yourself if you'd known what it was."

She put her hands to her head. "What—what racket? You're talking in riddles...."

"It's really very simple. You see, at the time you sold that movie theater to your husband and he in turn sold it to Mr. Deitz here, he was still an undischarged bankrupt out on the coast. Undischarged bankrupts can't buy and sell property. The deal was illegal. The property still belongs to you—and Mr. Dietz was very foolish to dump about ten million dollars' worth of building right on your land."

"You—you mean—I—that he—"

"Sure. You can stick him for plenty—that is, you could if you hadn't turned all your legal rights over to...."

I timed it just a fraction of a second too late.

The lacing jet of flame came from outside the bathroom window just as I went forward to my hands and knees and I felt it nick my collarbone. But my hat was off my gun now and I pounded four shots as fast as I could.

I heard a man yell. I roared at the girl and Dietz, "Stand right where you are!" and dived into the bathroom.

I slammed the door behind me to cut off light, sent the

window banging to the top. No more shots came. On the roof just outside the window, I saw a dark, huddled figure, slumping, heard harsh breathing. I eeled myself through the window and jumped.

I RAN TOWARDS him, squirting light from my flash—and that madness just about cost me my life. I had only time to see, in the glare of the momentary beam, Michigan Fahey, down on his knees, his hands crushed to his chest.

Then the gun spoke from the rear of the roof, and the flashlight exploded in my hands. Glass stung my face and three more vicious, slamming slugs jumped at me from the dark. I jerked my own gun up, squeezed lead twice. There was silence. Then I heard metal clang. I jumped up and ran to the edge of the roof. Flame lanced up at me once more from the fire-escape landing two floors below. I emptied my gun over the roof edge.

The dark figure cried out once, spun out over the fire-escape railing and went pitching, slowly turning, down into the back yard to land with a crash.

Sparks yelled from below: "My God—who is it?"

"Paul Muhl, the lawyer."

I ran back and knelt down beside the writhing, groaning little ex-convict, Fahey. "What'd he do? Fire at me and then put one in you?"

His words came in a sob through clenched teeth. "Yes, the ——."

"What in God's name did you let him use you in his racket for? Didn't you know he was just using you as a front—as a clay pigeon to attract all the suspicion while he really did the killing?"

"I—didn't know—at first. He offered me five grand to brace you like I did. It seemed like all the money in the world. He promised to hide me out if—if there was any heat. Get me out of town. I didn't know he was going to—knock anybody off. After last night, it was too late. I—he hadn't paid me. I dassent go on the street or the coppers would plug me. I had to do what he told me—"

"How'd he get on to the racket? Did you leave something in that apartment that he found when he moved in? Or—"

"I—when I stuck up Nirdlinger, I took a wallet off him. There were some letters in it—besides the bonds. I hid it in the bathroom—in the mirror on the cabinet. When I got out there was still one bond in it. I was desperate for a stake. He smashed in and—he caught me. He read the letters and propositioned me—*Ahhh*, God, my guts are gone...!"

Torch-beams lashed up over the edge of the roof as bluecoats and detectives swarmed around me. I yelled: "Get this one to a hospital, fast!"

I went back and climbed in through the girl's window, forcing her and Dietz back into the living-room. They were both starch-faced as I picked up my hat and knocked the dents out of it.

"Now you two can get together, without any middle man. Incidentally, when Muhl came to you and got you to put yourself entirely in his hands, how the hell did he work it? Why would you deal with a louse like him?"

She put a hand to her throat and swallowed. "He—he guaranteed me—ten thousand dollars. I didn't know it was anything like this. I thought it was just that accident when I was passing the building. I didn't realize that he—he had made me sign over *all* my legal rights, till…" She swallowed. "The… the agreement guaranteed me that much, plus twenty-five percent of anything he got for me above that."

I put my hat on thoughtfully, went out and called the chief and told him all.

"I still don't frame," I couldn't resist telling him.

Death in the Pluperfect

Her name was Eve, but it wasn't any Garden of Eden in which she found herself the night Glafke got himself perforated by an air-gun and she had to improvise both words and music for a three-way alibi—between appearances at the mike.

WHEN I SAW this Glafke that night, I was on the way to the high spot of my evening rounds—Eve Michaelson's eleven o'clock turn at the Trianon Club. I saw him when I strolled around from Broadway into Forty-eighth—the stunted little block that connects Seventh and Broadway where the avenues are only eighty-odd feet apart. He was standing under the tiny marquee of the Trianon's side door with Soldier Hambly, the doorman. The Soldier was planted in front of him, fists on hips, and I came round just in time to see him make a downward slashing gesture of finality with one white-gloved hand. Then he turned his back to go into the club.

Glafke put his chin down and said something short and harsh. He was a snake-hipped Latin-looking individual in smooth mustard-colored clothes, with a smooth gray face and black-rimmed staring brown eyes. He had an unlighted cigarette in his thin lips and it bobbed with his words.

The Soldier paused with the door open, turned his head over his shoulder to listen, then replied with one emphatic, sibilant syllable and went on in. Glafke snatched the cigarette from his lips, showing yellow teeth, hesitated a minute, glaring at the closed door. Then he turned angrily on his heel and strode for the corner beyond.

I put my mind on him for a minute—but only a minute. He was not a Broadway specimen. Harlem was more his beat. He was a cheap hustler, a mack, a lush-roller any time he got the chance, a shill for a couple of penny-ante Harlem shysters, and a peddler of marihuana cigarettes. Nothing about him would interest me in the slightest as a rule, but because of a certain current situation the last item gave him a momentary—even if very vague—claim on my consideration.

The situation was strictly Broadway. Ten days ago Dorinne Hale, the breathtaking little redheaded coat-checker from Mardi's restaurant, had been picked up on an East River pier more dead than alive. Things had been done to her clothes and her. She was black and blue from head to foot, her skull was fractured—and she was coked to the ears on marihuana. She was now in the hospital, with the best doctors in the city giving her the business, but the chances were a thousand to one that, if she did live, she would spend the rest of her days in an insane asylum. That, of course, mean as it was, was none of the Broadway Squad's business, because both Mardi's and the place where she was found were well outside our sector.

But Big George Polakoff suddenly appeared in the picture to give us all a case of galloping jitters. It developed that the redhead belonged to him—causing, incidentally, plenty nervousness among those who had tried passes at the girl at one time or another, which included practically every potent male on Broadway—and the big bruiser went berserk.

WE WOULD RATHER have had almost anybody in New York go berserk than Big George. He was one of the vanishing race—a real tough hoodlum. He had the town's labor-trouble strong-arm racket—services supplied to either side, and sometimes both—in the hollow of his thick, hairy hands. And although, now that he was a "business" man and draped his squat body in two-hundred-dollar suits, employed a

*As I came around the corner
Glafke backed into me.*

barber twice a day to scrape his thick jaw, part his coarse black
hair in the middle and oil it down—although he dallied with
sunlamp treatments, manicures, Florida vacations, even an
operation to remove a wen from the lid of one cold gray-blue
eye—he was still a life-taker at heart. Furthermore, he had an
array of "mediators" on his pay roll who were as vicious and
deadly a collection of thugs as any old-time mob ever assem-
bled. And, naturally, he had connections. He was a one-man
avalanche that even we couldn't stop.

He had it figured that somebody had slicked the girl into
a bang at the hay in order to interest her in other matters
and he was going to tear New York apart, paving-block by
paving-block, till he found out who. His plan, in general, was
to work over every peddler of the stuff in town, one by one,
till he shook the answer out of somebody. The big half-crazed

gorilla couldn't seem to understand that marihuana is a different proposition from heroin and morphine. H and M are both imported and can be checked, ounce by ounce, from importer to user. Marihuana can be, and is, raised in window-boxes and backyards, is no organized business but a hundred or a thousand unconnected little businesses, and to locate all the sellers of the stuff would take an army years. Even the chief, Marty Marquis—Lieutenant Marquis, my boss on the Broadway Squad—couldn't make Big George see that. He was going to locate every retailer in New York and squeeze a song out of one of them and that was all there was to it.

At that we had no particular objection as long as he didn't start playing bull-in-a-china-shop in our precincts. Unfortunately, Broadway was his most logical field and in his present mood, he and his mob were like to start dropping corpses or near-corpses, all over our landscape. Our earnest—if faint—hope was that a miracle would occur and his man turn up before trouble started, so we could persuade Big George to take him far, far out of the district and do his killing elsewhere. It was, I admit, so feeble that it couldn't really be called a hope at all, but naturally we were all painfully interested at the moment in *any*body we knew to be a peddler—even down to punks like Glafke.

However, after a mammoth effort of mind, I stopped making a fool of myself trying to think him into the star role in this picture. The unpleasant truth was that we were practically certain we'd eventually turn up a Broadway guy. It had that kind of smell.

Yet somehow, eliminating Glafke as a candidate for that particular mess didn't remove the pasty-faced Latin from my mind as I strolled on over to the club. He hung around in my head, until it began to puzzle me why. Along with my red hair I'm supposed to have one of those merciless memories, but I began foggily to wonder if I wanted this Glafke for some *other* job that I'd forgotten, or something like that.

The Soldier was off somewhere when I pushed under the Trianon's marquee, and I shouldered my way down the corridor and into my usual spot in one of the arched doorways of the packed blue-and-silver supper-room. I was a few minutes late and Eve Michaelson was already working. She pushed Glafke out of my mind, all right.

MOTIONLESS, SHE SAT in the darkened room, in a blue spot, on the piano. She sat with her hands folded in her lap, leaning a little forward, while she gave out with that silver-blue voice that a score of would-be imitators had nearly gone crazy trying to ape ever since she had first brought it to Broadway.

She was definitely not "flesh." She had a lovely, trim-waisted, slender body, neither short nor tall, beautifully curved where it should be, but she wore a simple evening gown of royal blue that sparkled faintly and had no other decoration. She was daintiness and grace. Her face was wistful, heart-shaped, her eyes deep blue. She wore her onyx-black hair in page-boy bob and her skin was like cream against it. But her song was her offering, not her body. She could take a standard torch ballad and send it out so that it went clear down inside you and bent your heart back and forth like a piece of rubber, leaving you choked up and blowing your nose for dear life. She did it like no one else could.

For the six or seven minutes that she worked, I went into a

mooning trance in which I had no mind for anyone as crass as Big George Polakoff and his girl, or Glafke, or anything else but the lovely little figure in front of me.

No, I wasn't in love with her, or on the make for her, or anything like that. She deserved, and had gotten, something far better than a dog-eared Broadway cop—to be exact, a Park Avenue doctor, by report a swell gent. Just call me an enthusiastic fan, on and off stage. So far from carrying the torch for her, I had been holding my breath for three years, rooting for her marriage to turn out right. She was a rare treasure in the up-all-night business—an artist who was really an artist, a dainty, warm, honest-to-God little person who knew all the answers in the book, and yet who had made her way strictly by offering talent and personality—and not a thing else.

She had registered solidly as long ago as '31, in the first couple of years that I was on the Squad—so solidly that a three-year layoff had not dimmed her drawing power one whit. For up till a week ago, she had been away for three full years, getting her marriage going. But she could, and did, step back instantly into the star spot in the Trianon, one of the town's three best clubs without a struggle. And there never was an empty chair, much less a table, at any of her three nightly appearances. The whole street was crazy about her, and me along with them, but get it straight once and for all that it was no Romeo proposition. I just liked to sit around and think what a swell gal she was, and relish every note of her three-song performance.

Presently, when the last thundering applause after her final number died away, I came reluctantly out of my daze. Presently I wandered out again to go about my business.

Then the ugly little thing closed in.

SOLDIER HAMBLY WAS just darting to the curb to pry open a limousine as I emerged. He saw me from the corner of his eye and shot hastily over his shoulder, "Ace—wait a second," and then, when he had attended to his duties, pulled me a few yards down the street. "There was a cheap little chiseler here a while ago. Name of Glafke."

"Yeah. I saw you barbering. What about him?"

"Well, he wanted to see Miss Michaelson. I told him to git, that I wouldn't carry messages from such as him. So he gets very tough. He says tell her she *better* see him if she knows what's good for her, and I chase him."

It slid under my skin like a cold needle. Stupid? Mister, I know Broadway. I smelt shakedown instantly. And—if you must know—worry about something like that was exactly what had *had* me holding my breath for three years about Eve. A cheap punk? Couldn't do her any harm? Brother, only a cheap punk *could* do her any harm. Only a cheap punk could know anything about her that I didn't know—a cheap punk out of the part of her career that had gone before I met her. Don't mistake me. She was tops to me, the essence of loveliness and integrity. But—she was a girl. She had come from a small town in Pennsylvania when she was eighteen and she had been on Broadway for six years, bucking it alone. That she had ever intentionally done anything dishonorable, or crooked, or rotten, was out of the question. But six years alone on Broadway would muck up the viewpoint of any girl who ever lived. There were things she might easily have slipped into that were none of those, but that might crucify her now. Understand. Nothing she could have done would damage her in my eyes one iota. But—I am not a Groton-Harvard-Johns-Hopkins-

Social Registerite. I am just a mopy Broadway cop who knows how it goes.

I'll admit that maybe I got a little overexcited in jumping to the unproved conclusion that the rat really had something. But what could I lose that way? There was only one possible thing to do anyway. Get my hands on him instantly and see where things stood. If he were running a phony or a bluff, I could kick his behind up through his shoulders and let it go at that. If he had something, the proper medicine was to get to him fast and take it away from him.

I clipped at the Soldier: "Where? Did he say where she should see him?"

"Huh?"

"Did Glafke leave any address where she should get in touch with him?"

"No. No. Look—he's over there—hangin' around there across the street, a little piece up the block there. See him? Readin' that slip of paper. Oops—there he goes, into a cab. Musta changed his mi…."

I got my hot eye on the pasty-faced Latin, a quarter of a block beyond the corner opposite, just as he crowded into a Checker. I took three quick strides and then the Checker shot away and I realized I had no chance on foot. Two silk-hatted youngsters were stepping into a cab at the very corner beside me. I brushed them aside, snarling, "Police business," at them, and, to the cabby, "Get your eye on that Checker up ahead. Catch it."

This Charlie Cowlishaw, the bespectacled, silvery-blond-haired tabloid reporter came round the corner and stopped, just as I jumped in and we shot forward. I spared him one dizzy mental curse and a quick prayer that he had not seen or heard me, but I really had no mind for him at that moment.

THEN WE LOST Glafke. We were caught squarely in the after-theater jam and he was half a block ahead of us in the choking swarm of taxis. We could just keep him in sight while we worried and squealed and snarled across to Sixth, to Fifth. Then he caught a traffic-light that we missed—not that a light would have stopped us if we had been where we could get through, but we were pinned behind six other cars. The jam did not extend beyond Madison and he got clear and away. I didn't think the pup even knew he was being chased.

I exhausted my vocabulary on my driver, although I couldn't blame him a hell of a lot, and we spent thirty useless minutes doubling back and forth up the east side of town—both of us had the cab's license number in mind, of course—before we finally gave up.

I had him drive me back across to Broadway—we were up at Fiftieth street—and I dropped off at the corner. The drug store of the Bryant Hotel was across from me and I stood on the curb, wondering if there was any reason why I shouldn't put out some of my regular wires to locate the white-faced Latin. I decided there wasn't and stepped out, just a second too late, the lights having changed on the instant—and stared straight into a cab window at Glafke.

And in the very instant of recognition, he was away. The cab must have been standing feet from me, for minutes, but I had not glanced into its interior till the moment when it zoomed away and it was far out of reach by the time I reacted to make a grab for it.

And that fantastic slip let the whole thing plunge out of control.

I flagged another cab, was into it and shooting after him in seconds, of course. He had freer going here, but so did we. I still didn't think he knew I was after him.

For the first time, the possibility that he might have a head man, that he was just somebody's hired hand, occurred to me suddenly and I snapped at my driver: "Take it easy. Don't catch him—just tail…."

Glafke's cab swerved into the curb at that moment, just a quarter-block below the corner of Fifty-fourth. I said hastily, "Whoa—right here," and we stopped, fifty feet behind him.

I waited till he got out and paid his driver and was well on his way to the corner above before I went after him. He didn't look back as he turned the corner and the minute he was out of sight I broke into a half-trot.

I was twenty or thirty feet from the corner when the queer pounding noise sounded ahead of me. I speeded up and swung around the corner.

Glafke backed into me. He was bent over almost double and I was going too fast to stop. Hastily I had to throw both arms around him to keep him from being butted down on his head. He had his hands grinding into his face. He was making a sound like sobbing and he suddenly collapsed in my arms like a sack of wheat. I was almost pulled down myself and had to let go of him to keep my balance. He suddenly screamed and started rolling around, kicking the pavement with his heels, till I could dive down and yank him over on his back. Then I saw the black stuff streaming over his hand and I jerked out my flashlight and touched the button. The black stuff was red.

It was blood and I hastily yanked and pulled till I got his hand away from his face. As I did his screaming dropped down to a spine-chilling, guttural whining, as he went on throwing himself about.

His right eye was completely gone. The eye-socket was just a terrible streaming hole.

Not till then did I get the significance of the noise I had heard—an air-pistol. Somebody had been waiting round that corner for Glafke and had let him have a slug square in the eye. I felt my heart turn over.

I DROPPED HIM, jumped up, located my whistle, jammed it in my mouth and blew. I ran out, my eyes straining into the middle of the roadway and across the street, back again. It was a black, narrow little street, lined with towering dark apartment buildings and there were cars parked solidly at both sides of the curb.

I saw a doorman hurry out from the nearest building and look curiously toward me. Other than that there wasn't a single moving figure between me and the nearest bright light a block and a half away. I snapped at the doorman, "Call an ambulance—life and death," and he made a funny spread-legged jump and turned and ran back into his building. The shot man was now moaning feebly, barely moving himself about and I was reluctant to leave him, but I ran a few yards up the street, peering behind parked cars, still blowing my whistle.

I saw no killer, or anyone that could be suspected as a killer. Even looking became useless almost immediately, as people began funnelling out of the buildings. The air-pistol marksman was away clean.

Two sirens started keening, racing toward me from opposite directions.

I guess it was the clanging of the ambulance bell, however, that snapped me back to frightened sanity. Who...?

No mental strangling in the world could keep my mind away from Eve Michaelson, of course. Could the moaning, unconscious rat at my feet have really had something, had he somehow contacted the girl, had...?

I had just time to get through searching him—hastily and fruitlessly—before the two sirening prowl cars screamed in to the curb almost as one, and bluecoats piled out. I opened my mouth to snap at them—and from the corner of my eye I saw a taxi slide in to the curb and catatpult out onto the sidewalk the owlish, bespectacled dumpy little reporter, Charlie Cowlishaw.

From then on, all I wanted to do was get away from there. I growled at the prowl-car-sergeant: "I was just walking along and heard something that sounded like an air-pistol. This lug backed into me and started to wrestle with me and by the time I found what it was all about, there was no sign of who did it."

I couldn't make a quick break, of course—not an obvious one. But when the ambulance clanged up and the white-coated internes ran over and mulled over the shot man, I eased to the back of the crowd. I could just hear them say: "...won't last till we get him to the hospital...."

I turned to slip away—and found the dumpy little Cowlishaw beaming up at me. Somehow he had slipped around behind me. He had grape-blue eyes as big as plums behind his spectacles and he looked like a friendly cocker-spaniel. He said softly: "Now isn't that a coincidence. You take off after...."

"Did you ever hear the story about the reporter who was

found with his head in a bucket of cement?" I asked him grimly, and when that got a pinched look on his face, I walked past him. I was a damn long way from being sure it would hold him—some of these reporters have no sense at all—but it was a thousand times more important that I get something else solid first. I snagged a cab and raced back to the Trianon.

I DON'T KNOW if I expected to find that some evil genii had spirited Soldier Hambly away from the side door or not, but I sweated with relief when the cab dumped me in front of him. His eyes went big when he saw my face. I guess I was sweating a little from all the running around. I palmed his coat front.

"Get this and get it right. You never saw Glafke tonight. He wasn't around here. You never mentioned him to me."

He swallowed and nodded quickly. "O—O.K. Did—did you...?" he whispered.

"I didn't do anything."

I strode past him and into the supper-room. My watch said five minutes to twelve and I knew Eve wasn't on again till one. I grabbed a captain and said in his ear: "Take me back to Miss Michaelson's dressing-room quickly—and no back talk."

He gulped, "Well, sure, Mr. McGuire," and led me around a hall behind the orchestra dais. The dressing-rooms were up a flight of stairs on a little balcony and when we got to the top of the stairs he pointed to another hall and said: "There—the fourth."

I didn't knock till he had gone down again and my heart was in my mouth when I did, but her voice called, "Come in," and I went in.

A look at her face frightened me. She was still lovely, look-ing twenty instead of her twenty-six or -seven, graceful and dainty. Her face had the glow that comes after freshly removed make-up, but it also had two little spots that looked like fever, high on her cheekbones. Her blue eyes looked at me—and lighted up. She had a glass of champagne in one hand and she quickly put it down and held out both her hands to me. "Why—Ace! How nice. This is Mr. McGuire of the Broadway Squad, Dick, one of the finest cops money can buy."

A tall youngster, almost painfully thin, with electric black eyes and a thin, sensitive mouth, also put down a glass of champagne and disentangled his long legs from two chairs. He was a fine-looking kid and I knew who he was—her husband's son by a former marriage. He was a violinist—not an orchestra one, but the kind that appears in Carnegie Hall—that is, he would be, they hoped, when he got through studying. He made me a little bow and fumbled till I held out my hand. Then he smiled a little embarrassedly. "I—I'm just waiting for Dad, you know."

I didn't get what he meant for a second and then I realized the dope was embarrassed—or thought he should be—at being in Eve's dressing-room. It was gruesomely funny....

Or was it? I was wild-eyed enough to even think of *that*—that some monkey-business might be going on here—that *that* might have been Glafke's ammunition. The kid would be about twenty... his father must be over forty... Eve was closer to the youngster's age then... and the kid, for all his Park Avenue, was a musical genius or something and maybe erratic.... Could something like this be what Glafke...?

Yeah, I was plenty fatuous there for a minute. I said, "Eve—

could I see you a second," and the kid took the hint, started toward the door.

She frowned and searched me anxiously with her deep-blue eyes. "Why, don't be silly, Ace. Dick and I are close friends. There can't be anything you'd ask me that I wouldn't want him to hear. Don't go, Dick."

I ran a finger around inside my collar. "Well, I was just going to ask you if you were out a little while ago," I said finally.

Her eyes wondered on mine. "Out? How do you mean?"

"I mean out of the club—say in the last half-hour. Or three-quarters."

She looked worried and bewildered. "No. I haven't." Then as I opened my mouth again, she looked flusteredly toward the blinking youngster. "Dick's been here longer than three-quarters of an hour, haven't you, Dick? It must be that long. He'll assure you I haven't been out."

He did just that.

Until I got out again, I almost sweated with relief. I passed it off with some gag about having seen someone on the street that looked like Eve and having been royally high-hatted when I spoke to her.

Once it became apparent that it *wasn't* Eve who had killed Glafke, that she had a sound little alibi, I wanted to kick myself around the block for my feverish vaporings. I gagged and wisecracked till I got them grinning and then I bowed out.

THE MINUTE I was outside, miserable logic reminded me that she was an actress, and that the kid would certainly lie if he thought she wanted—or needed—him to. So I doublechecked.

I went out to Harry Driggs, the doorman on the front door

and asked him: "How long was Miss Michaelson out, just a little while ago?"

He blinked. "She didn't come out my way, Ace. She always uses the Soldier's door.... No, I ain't been off the door for a minute myself."

When I went back to the Soldier I said: "Be damn careful what you tell me. I want to know exactly when Miss Michaelson went out and how long she was gone."

His red Irish pan got anxious. "Not by me, Ace. She never come out by me."

"What's the longest you been away from the door since I was here?"

"Two minutes," he said promptly. "The chef always sends me up some coffee at eleven-thirty and I gotta get out of sight to drink it. She couldn't of gone out and come in in two minutes." That closed the gate for me. It was air-tight.

There was still one other angle, but I didn't really go for it, and anyway it was cleared up for me almost automatically.

It occurred to me and I asked the Soldier suddenly: "What's Miss Michaelson's husband's name again? Her married name?"

"Van Decker. Doctor Van Decker."

"What's their address, do you know?"

"Yeah, but if you want *him*, he's in the bar."

"What?"

"Yeah, he came in about half an hour ago. At least half an hour ago. And some drunk collared him as he was passing the bar and dragged him in. I just noticed he hadn't got away yet."

I went back quickly and into the chromium-and-flamingo, bar. It was fairly crowded, but not jammed.

I saw Van Decker at the end of the bar, and I saw the jam

he was in. He had the same black eyes as his son and the same dark-brown hair, but his sensitive face was tolerant and appreciative, rather than intense. He was smiling and being friendly to two fat little drunks in evening clothes who had their arms around him. I could hear their conversation in patches.

"… wouldn't be 'live today except for old Ralph here… already had two operations… given me up… four hours on the table… good as new… old Ralph here…."

I stepped down to the opposite end of the bar and managed to catch the bartender's eye.

"Has the doctor been here ever since he came in, Ted?" I asked when he came down.

He grinned and swabbed the bar. "Yeah, and it looks like he'll be here all night with that pair."

He wasn't there all night. He broke away, just as I made for the door and as he was closer, we went through almost together. I knew him slightly and, although I don't think he placed me, my redhead must have seemed familiar to him for he gave me a faint rueful smile and a friendly look from his dark eyes as we passed out.

It wasn't a murderer's smile.

And he wasn't a murderer. His alibi just barely covered the time element, but it did cover it positively, and it, too, was air-tight.

Why was I worried? Despite my absolute checking off of the only three that I was worrying about, there was still the tight little fright in my middle. I tried groggily to grope out why? Was there some little drama here under my very nose that I was missing? And what if there was? Who cared—as long as these three were completely unconnected with the shooting of Glafke? What the hell was eating me?

There was only one thing to do in a case like that. I beat it down to the Theater Ticket Agency on Times Square that is more or less the headquarters of the Broadway Squad and told the whole works to the Marquis.

HE WAS ALONE in the place, sitting behind a desk, neat, dapper in black Chesterfield, tight black silk muffler and black hard hat. He linked his little black-gloved hands across his tummy and eyed me curiously with his shaded China-blue eyes, for nearly three minutes, after I had finished.

Of course he didn't get to be lieutenant of the Broadway district, handling the toughest, meanest, shrewdest thieves in the business—and the biggest single concentration of them in the business—without a keen head on him. But he was way off line this time when he said in his quiet voice: "Ordinarily you're a pretty wide-awake cop, Ace. But you're so damned hungry for this girl yourself—plus being excitable anyway— that you're all confused here."

"I'm not after her, if that's what you mean," I told him. "But O.K., so I'm confused. What the hell am I worried about?"

"The newshawk for one thing," he said as he lifted himself out of the chair. "The way you tell it, he must have overheard you spill that you were after Glafke when you took off from the Trianon the first time—or talked to someone who did. Then he finds you bending over the punk's dead body. You can't just hope you scared him and that he stays scared. We'll have to build up a story to satisfy him."

"What story?"

"Come on. We're going places. The story isn't so hard."

He pointed out what we could say, as we walked the few

blocks to the gaudy skyscraper Medallion Hotel, and I wondered why I hadn't thought of it myself. A little while back, I mentioned a situation that we had on Broadway at this time, involving Big George Polakoff and his redheaded girl—how she evidently got in the hands of somebody with marihuana and was now so close to death that it had the big strong-arm guy nearly out of his head. And also that this Glafke, the murdered man, off and on, did some business in the weed. Well, whereas it hadn't been reasonable enough for me to credit, still it tied together well enough to choke off the newspapers.

We went into the thick-rugged, gold-and-crystal lobby of the Medallion, rode twenty-two floors and knocked on Big George Polakoff's door.

He was evidently alone in the suite. He came to the door with a glass of amber-colored fluid in his hand, his suspenders dangling to his knees and his shirt off. His beefy, big-jawed face was muddy and twitching, his black-browed ice-gray eyes red-streaked and feverish. When he recognized us, he said dully: "Oh. Coppers. Well, come in."

We went in. He had been hitting the bottle plenty from the evidence. "Well, whaddaya want?"

The Marquis looked round at the litter of bottles and asked, "Have you any beer? Do you mind if I order some up?" and when the big giant grunted, he stepped to the phone and told room service to rush some.

He asked Polakoff, unhurriedly: "Do you know a bird named Glafke?"

"No."

The Marquis nodded absently, as though he were confirming something he already knew. He asked Polakoff gently if he had learned anything new about... *that*... and the big giant almost cracked. He threw down his glass and went into a crazy, half-sobbing stream of profanity and wild threats that were interrupted only by the knocking on the door of the boy with the beer.

The Marquis told me, "Get it and give him a dollar," and I did.

The Marquis set the bottle on the table, talked soothingly for a minute or two, then said, "Well, you know how we feel, George. Let us know if there's anything we can do," and we went out.

When we were in the hall, I said: "What the hell is this?"

"The bellhop will be spreading the news that you and I were in Big George's room within an hour of the time Glafke was killed. We say nothing from now on and the very brilliant newshawks can beat their brains out against it just as it stands."

When we got back to the Agency, he said: "O.K., now. It's your case and I give it back to you. Just keep your lips buttoned and you're all right. You'll have to stand off Homicide and maybe the Narcotic Squad but they won't be losing much sleep over a punk like that. The papers will make up their minds that Big George tagged Glafke for the attack on his checkroom girl and the thing will die a natural death."

IT DID—ALMOST. FOR the first few days, I nearly got a stiff neck wagging my head, no, no comment, and some of the boys from headquarters made some loud growls. But after the second week it was out of the papers entirely and only the columnists were taking odd cracks at it.

And yet something was eating me. I couldn't go near Eve

Michaelson. She stayed, week after week, at the Trianon, but I no longer felt like going in to catch her numbers. I couldn't figure why. Then, suddenly, it all blasted open.

I was in the Agency, it so happened, when my phone rang at one in the morning.

I don't know how I recognized the voice, because I had only seen the kid the once in my life, but I knew it was young Dick Van Decker. He blurted out hoarsely: "Mr. McGuire?"

"Yeah."

"Well, listen. If you want to know who killed that Glafke, I can tell…" and then there was a loud sound like a door closing.

I yelled, "Hello, hello," but I got no answer. I yelled at one of the others in the Agency, "Trace this—I've still got it open…" and the receiver at the other end was quietly hung up.

I looked wildly around for the Marquis. He was out at the moment.

I jumped up as big Johnny Berthold called, "Here y'are," and scribbled on a piece of paper. I threw at them as I ran for the door: "If the Marquis comes in, have him wait for me."

I glanced at the slip as I piled into a cab and read, *R. Van Decker. Studio 19, 157a W. Fifty-seventh St.,* and I sweated blood while we raced up there.

It was an old building, with an automatic elevator and a lobby open to the street and deserted. I charged in with no one to stop me and luckily found a board inside the car that told me Studio 19 was on the fourth floor. I ran off into a dimly lit, long mahogany hall whose rubber runner barely changed the tone of my footsteps. I saw that Studio 19 was the only one in the row with its transom lighted, and I had my gun in my hand when I grabbed the knob.

I didn't need any gun. The unlatched door flew open under my push. The studio was hardly furnished at all—a couch against the wall, a piano, a few music racks and some piles of sheet music, a chair. The telephone sat primly on a little shelf just large enough to hold it, over the head of the couch.

Young Van Decker lay white and still on the couch in dinner clothes, his legs trailing on the floor. There was a jagged hole in his left temple, from which blood had veined down his cheek. There was not much blood and it was already drying.

An air-pistol lay on the piano.

For one second, I stood without breathing. Then I swung the door to behind me and jumped for him, grabbed for his pulse.

THE PULSE WAS still beating, regularly, fairly strong. I couldn't think what to do. I reached for the phone to call an ambulance—but I couldn't make myself do it. I wasn't thinking rationally, I guess, but the only thing that beat over and over in my mind was that he might talk. And if he talked—who could he name but Eve Michaelson? He could not possibly know of any other killer except Eve—whose alibi he had falsified. Or could he? Could it be that he had somehow dug up some information somewhere else—that the alibi he had given her was legitimate?

But my heart sank at the prospect of gambling on that.

I could feel sweat beading my forehead. I tried to look at his wound, but apart from the fact that the skin was broken on his temple I could not tell much. The clotted blood obscured anything else. Yet if there were an air-pistol slug in his brain....

I thought of the Marquis finally. I groaned at my own brainstorm and jumped for the phone....

The door opened quickly, closed as quickly behind me, and the Marquis walked swiftly in.

I blurted: "My God—how...?"

His round little Santa-Claus face was tight and intent, his blue eyes sweeping the prone boy. "Big Johnny told me where you'd gone. I came to keep you from making a fool of yourself." He was already beside the boy, had his fingers darting from the unconscious youth's pulse to his temple-wound.

I stammered: "He—he called me. He told me he could name the one who killed Glafke. He was shot before he could finish. —— —— it, Marty—she must have done it—and killed Glafke too."

"Don't be an..." he started.

There was a hand fumbling at the door. The Marquis dived toward it.

The door came open, but I could not see who was outside because the Marquis interposed. A quiet voice said: "I guess I am the man you want...."

The door was shut in my face. The Marquis had gone out through it and closed it behind him so quickly that I was left with my mouth open. I jumped across the room, grabbing for the knob—but I didn't grab. On the Broadway Squad, you learn early not to question the Marquis' moves and habit handcuffed me.

Even as I hesitated, he came quickly and nimbly back into the room, closed the door and put his back to it. He said, "Go over and see if that phone works," and when I found it did, he rattled off a number for me to call.

I dialed with sweating fingers, trying to read the answer in his face. My hair nearly stood on end when the voice answered in my ear: "Hotel Medallion. Good-morning."

I opened my mouth—and he took the phone away from me. "Give me Mr. Polakoff's suite, quickly. Police business," he said, and then as I tried to get out a question, he snapped, "Shut up."

A second later, he said: "Big George? This is Marty Marquis. Yeah… Well, maybe. But let's see if we've got everything straight now. You're not forgetting? Your risk… Kidnaping… Cement?… All right, I'm at Studio 19, the Carnoba Studios on Fifty-seventh. Yeah. Keep your head now and play it out the way we… Yeah."

He hung up instantly. I burst, "What… what…?" but he grabbed my arm and steered me firmly toward the door. "Keep your trap shut and let's get out of here."

HE RUSHED ME downstairs and we ran half a block before we could flag a cab, then he snarled me to silence savagely as we drove back to the Agency. Not till we were safely in the back room, alone, did he turn on me.

"What in God's name?" I raved. "That kid—may be dying—leave him there—Big George…?"

"Big George will take care of him," the Marquis said. "Big George is anxious to take care of him."

"My God—you don't mean…?"

"Sure. I mean he fixed Big George's redhead. Probably they both were full of weed and he's one of those that it drives batty. Maybe there could be a way out for him on that, though I doubt it, but—certainly there's no out for him on the murder of Glafke."

"Glafke!"

"Yes, yes," he said impatiently. "Glafke must have been the one that sold him the stuff. Glafke must have nosed out the truth—or enough of it so that he started looking for the kid to put him on the shake. The kid got wind of it and knew he was on the spot, so he lost his head and knocked Glafke off. Then he ran to Eve Michaelson for cover. That night when you thought she was in the soup and that he was giving her an alibi, it was the other way round, stupid. She gave *him* one. How? Hell, that's easy. She knew the Soldier went for his coffee every night at a certain hour and she had the kid wait outside till that hour and then duck in, come up to her room. Then she claimed he'd been there all along."

"But... who shot the kid tonight?"

He looked at my middle button and took a long, slow breath. "Son, I hate to tell you this, but I'm afraid you're not in the running in that family.

"The kid—you have only to look at him to know he's ripe meat for trouble, for wild stuff. The very fact that she wasn't too shocked to cover him up for murder argues that she must be used to it—that he must have got in jams before, although nobody's heard of it. But evidently his father is fond of the kid and she went to bat that night to spare the doctor the final blow. She made herself an accessory to murder to do it. Realize that. Mark it down. She made herself an accessory to first-degree murder. She could burn! That's why I clammed up at the time—till I could arrange things."

"Clammed up? You mean you knew?"

"I didn't *know*, no. But I had a damn good idea. Once I thought of him in connection with Big George's redhead, the rest was fairly reasonable. No?"

"Yes, yes. But—but tonight...?"

"Tonight, the young louse decided to confess."

It was a full minute before the full, shattering implication of that dawned on me. "Good God—then she…?"

"Certainly. She would burn along with him. That's why I turned him over to Big George—as per my agreement."

I sat down and put my hands to my head. Then I suddenly jumped up. "But when his body's found—there'll be a new stink—maybe if Big George messes him up, the Homicide or Narcotic guys will connect it all up.…"

"They couldn't prove anything if they did, as far as that goes. Glafke's dead, the kid's dead. Who can talk? Big George? Yes, but he won't. And anyway, the body won't be found. That was part of the agreement."

"What agreement?" I said wildly. "You've been talking about some agreement that— Wait, you mean you went to Big George before tonight…?"

"Of course. I got his promise—and it's good—that nobody will ever see the rat again. Big George knows he's going to have to face a kidnaping rap—or rather, a chase. I don't think they'll ever hang it on him, but he doesn't give a damn if they do. He wanted that kid like he never wanted anything in his life. When he's through with him, he goes into a barrel of cement and even if he is caught up with, Big George isn't the kind to talk. So everything's tidied up, son. What's the matter?"

"Matter?" I said hoarsely. "Nothing. Only I—she found out tonight that he was going to confess? And involve her? She went up there tonight to stop him—and tried to kill…?"

"No, stupid. Get that fever out of your head. *She* didn't do it. *He* did. Her husband. The doctor. The kid's father. He found out just at the last minute—yeah, that was him in the hall up there. He got there just as the kid was about to shoot off his face to you and plugged him, then ran out. But he got all full of ideals and figured how he could take the rap without telling why, so he came back. Get it? He was willing to kill his own son, rather than let Eve go over. That's why I say you're out in the cold, chum. Those folks kind of like each other. Now go on up and tell them their son's been kidnaped. Tell them to wait a couple of days before reporting it. Be careful how much you tell them."

I walked up to the Trianon. When I got there, somehow I still didn't want to go in. But I finally did.

Picture Killer

Big Johnny Berthold was the squad's muscle man and his mighty biceps extended well above his ears. One thing his skipper had tried to drill into his fat head was never to try to handle a homicide alone. But the temptation was too much for Johnny when his fighter pal got into a kill-frame. It took the whole Broadway Squad to get the dumb lug out of the grease—and the Marquis to turn him into a brain-guy for a night.

1

—

Set-Up for Slaughter

DURING THE EIGHTH bloody round it got so even I could see that the match should never have been made, that it was a lunatic's blunder. No matter what Danny Harmon had, he was too damned green to go against the crafty, ten-tricks-a-minute veteran Negro and the Negro had him practically cut to pieces. The Garden crowd was a howling, screaming mob. The stumbling, half-crazed kid could not possibly survive another three minutes of the vicious beating. He had been stagger-ing in a terrible blind punchfog since the fourth. I was numb, shocked—and empty inside as I looked over at Mary Harmon.

She was huddled there, her eyes black hollows in her starch-white little face, her lipstick jagged, the line of her soft, dark-red hair sharp against her skin. Her fingers were clenched like iron in her lap, but she still sat tight in her seat beside Wally Hewlett. I could see her trembling.

I was near crazy to get her out of the place, to have her not see any more of the slaughter. I tried to signal Wally, but I couldn't. His dark face was away from me, his worried black eyes down in their corners, watching her anxiously. Though I squirmed myself into sweating knots as the rest period raced away, I couldn't get his eye. Then the buzzer sounded and then the bell.

DANNY STOOD UP, reeled, staggered, and threw himself at the Negro. Only that seemed left in his bursting brain—

He plunged forward, a long-bladed knife in his hand.

to keep throwing himself. It was madness. The whistling haymaker he pitched two thirds of the way across the ring was the sucker punch of a novice. The sliding Negro's hard straight smash to the mouth stopped him cold. Only the fact that Danny's knees buckled and he stumbled, saved him from the vicious following right-cross. The thick-legged Negro bounced, was after him like lightning, cracked a left to the kid's jaw and rushed in, digging a thunderous right uppercut under his heart as he tied him up. He wrestled him around. Danny's face was bloody, senseless, desperate, one eye almost closed,

his black hair matted. The 'picture' fighter of his last fourteen fights was gone, his clean-limbed eager grace. The Negro had cuffed, elbowed, butted everything Sam Link had taught him clear out of his fevered head. Everything but heart. When the referee pried them apart, he almost fell—but he threw himself doggedly, sobbingly forward again.

Even the Negro was looking a little hunted. He chopped, chopped, broke ground, his icy little eyes baffled as the kid did not go down. He caught him coming in again, with a vicious right hook that knocked him clear across the ring and almost over the ropes, but the kid staggered drunkenly around, still upright.

Then the flash of white in Danny's corner caught my eye and I saw Sam Link's warped, bony-red, narrow, little face suddenly pop up. His face was twisted in a hell of agony—he had some vicious stomach trouble and was in the very act of cramming one of his interminable capsules into his mouth—but at long last he had the towel in his hand and he flung it desperately.

How Danny's pain-blinded eyes saw it, God knows, but they did. He saw it and made an instant, staggering dive for it. Somehow he caught it on the back of his hand, slapped it crazily out of the ring, swung drunkenly toward Sam Link— and the diving Negro nailed him. A terrific straight left behind the ear pitched the kid down like a sack of meal, crashed him on the apron of the ring—and Mary Harmon could stand no more. From the corner of my eye I caught just a flash of her as she ran out, stumbling blindly, sobbing, her hands over her face, up the aisle, Wally, juggling hats and coats, his fine, dark face intense, in anxious pursuit a second later.

Even if I could have taken my eyes from the ring, I could not have caught up with them. The Garden was in a screaming turmoil as the referee's arm swung, and the loud-speaker roared out the count. Through shoulders, I could see Danny down, like a blind, stunned animal, swaying, his gloves sprawled out, trying frantically to push himself up. He couldn't. Six... seven... He was sobbing, helpless... Eight... He made a feeble pawing grab at where he thought the ropes were—and the bell rang.

The final round—I'll skip it. The kid's hands hung practically at his sides after the first two seconds. The Negro simply whacked and punched him all over the ring. The thud, smash, the spray of blood and sweat from the ring almost drove me out of my mind. He was down four times, the last three in the final eight seconds. He ended up on one knee, tears streaming down his shapeless face, his body twitching with his terrible efforts to get up. There was barely a count at all. Then the bell hammered out and it was all over and the sensational reputation that Sam Link had carefully nursed and cooked for Danny for eighteen months was a joke. He had gone into the ring as the coming threat, an unstoppable picture fighter, on the way to the crown. He came out just another green possibility, on his way back to the bushes.

He wouldn't let me in his dressing-room afterwards.

Nor could I find Sam Link, although I hunted for him all during the eight-rounder windup, all over the Garden. Nobody had seen him, I was told.

I SAT GLOOMILY by myself in Dempsey's, making rings on a corner table with a highball glass. I'd been there for half an hour when Wally came wearily in, saw me, and dropped into a chair opposite me. His clean, fine-looking dark face was drawn and weary and his electric black eyes were reddened.

He signaled a waiter and said in a tired voice: "I hear he lasted."

"How's Mary?"

"She's all right. She's a wonderful girl, Johnny."

I licked my lips. "Did she—say anything about me?"

He looked at me cloudily. "No. Why should she say anything about you?"

His drink coming saved me answering. But he kept at me. "Haven't given her up entirely yet, eh, Johnny?"

I growled: "That's good—coming from you. I'm surprised you didn't attack her on the way home in the cab—if you didn't."

It brought back a sickly trace of good humor, even if it didn't mine. He got up a ghost of a smile! "She'd get better than that from me," he insinuated.

Don't get that wrong. Neither of us had a chance with her. Neither of us ever had had—although we had to learn it the hard way. I was in the hospital. A safe-and-loft mob had tried to shoot it out with me on Tenth Avenue and I was having their lead picked out, when I first saw her. Even a nurse's stiff white uniform and cap had not hidden her soft little curls, her milk-white skin and glowing red hair. She had starry, long-lashed eyes that were pansy-colored and after ten days, I was floundering.

So was Wally. I had known him since P.S. 45 and the safe-and-loft mob that had sprayed me had figured it smart to retain him as their lawyer. It was all right with him. He had no scruples about using his drag with me and he came to call to see if I would do business. Once he ran into her and I saw the hungry-eyed look come over him, I knew *I* was licked. His dark, fine good looks, with curly black hair and snapping black eyes—and me, overgrown, battered up, every knuckle of my hands broken at one time or another on some crook's jaw and scars all over me. On top of that, him a brilliant, rising lawyer, with a brain like a flash of lightning, and me—well, even my boss, the Marquis—Lieutenant Marquis to you—says I think like creeping paralysis. I knew *I* was out, right there.

The joke was—so was Wally out. When he started putting the business on her, she produced Danny Harmon, fresh from Golden Gloves, to ask my 'advice'. He wanted to go on the cops so they could get married. I talked him into postponing the cops till he found out did he have as many possibilities in his fists as I thought. I knew Sam Link—come to think of it, through Wally, whose client he was—and for my dough, Sam was the brains of the fight business. I put them in with each other.

Sam nursed him along like a baby for a year and a half, fighting him around the country, giving him high-pressure coaching, building him up, handpicking opponents and beating the drum for him like only Sam knew how. He had had him in every sports column in the country, headed for a title shot and a million-dollar gate—and then this. And tonight was the first and only time Mary had seen him in action. That's why I asked about did she say anything about me. See? I put him in the fight business to begin with. For all I knew, she might be putting it all on my head. That's why I asked.

I came out with the thing that was burning me up, blurted at Wally: "What happened to Sam's brains when he made this match? That colored boy is a washed-up second-rater that only knows dirty tricks. Why did Sam put the kid in there with him?"

Wally turned his glass slowly. "For dough, Johnny. The jig passed up nine tenths of the purse to get the shot. The kid's end is over twenty grand."

"There's no sense in that. Sam owns a night-club in town here, a summer hotel on the borscht circuit, a dog-track in Florida, that I know of—part of it anyways. And other things. He doesn't need money."

Wally said wearily, "Everybody, everywhere, always, needs m…" and stopped, his black eyes flicking upwards.

I looked up and saw Big Tim Donnelly. His red face was nipped by the cold and his gray eyes were ice under his straight black brows. He said in his slaty voice: "Hello, Johnny.... Where's Sam, Wally?"

Wally shrugged. "I wish I knew. I guess he doesn't feel much like seeing anybody tonight."

"I want to see him. Tell him if you see him," he said harshly and moved on.

I persisted at Wally: "Sam didn't need money that bad—not enough to set the kid's career back a whole year—maybe forever..." But he wasn't listening. He was staring after Big Tim with a queer thoughtful look in his electric black eyes. "Wha's matter?"

"Nothing. Nothing. I—" He hesitated and a line came in his dark forehead. "Somebody told me Big Tim was betting plenty on Danny being knocked out, that's all."

"Huh? Well, the louse," I said.

Then I saw Danny Harmon come in through the Eighth Avenue door, looking around. I stood up, warning Wally: "Ixnay, the kid."

THEY HAD DONE wonders with his face but it was still puffed and lumpy, a mouse on one eye and strips of adhesive on his cheeks. His neat gray overcoat hung open to show his dark suit and gray shirt and little black bow tie, and he carried his cap in his hand. His dark-blue eyes were bloodshot and beaten and he bobbed his head without looking up when people spoke to him. He was almost hangdog—till he saw my hand-wagging and came over. Even then he just edged up. He licked his lips and said huskily: "I—I'm sorry, Johnny. I done the—the best

I could. Is Sam…?"

I said heartily: "You were swell—don't let anybody tell you you weren't. The dirty rat got you with his head in the fourth or you'd of slaughtered him. Next time, you'll kill him."

The kid gulped and mumbled something. He twisted his cap. "You don't know where Sam is, do you fellows? He—he doesn't seem to be around anywhere I've looked."

The waiter, following Wally's quick signal, brought over a double Scotch and Wally said: "Forget Sam for tonight, Danny. Put this inside you and you'll feel better. Go on—I know all about what Sam would say. I'm his lawyer and I'm representing him. You rate this tonight. Drink it down. Go on, Danny."

The kid shifted from foot to foot, then, mainly because he couldn't figure out how to refuse, I guess, got the drink down. I said: "Yeah, forget Sam for tonight and go home to Mary, Danny."

"I am going home," he said huskily. "But I got to see Sam first. I—" There was a groping, frightened look in his eyes for a second. He swallowed. "Well—well thanks for the drink, Mr. Hewlett. I—I guess I better be going now."

After he had left, we sat gloomily in silence. Finally Wally shook his head and then said: "Let's go and drown our troubles at the Club Vincennes. What do you say?"

"Don't be silly. It's out of the Broadway district and I'd have to pay there. I couldn't afford a toothpick at that scatter."

"With every well-heeled crook in the business running to the other end of the country to escape this reform wave, I can't either. But a client of mine is throwing a party there tonight and I'm invited—with friend. Come on. This wake isn't helping anyone."

It was the lushest, most expensive spot on the East Side, with coconut palms, hula-hula dancers and crazy-sounding drinks at two bucks a copy. We stood it for three solid hours. It was around two thirty when we left and Wally drove me home in his block-long Cadillac convertible.

And then the blow-off.

The rooming-house in the West Eighties where I live calls itself a hotel because it has a postage-stamp lobby and a switch-board. When I waved goodnight to Wally and started up the steps, the night attendant popped his head out of his cubicle and said, "Oh—Mr. Berthold—a party just this minute rang off. Here—" He poked out a message slip at me.

I recognized Mary Harmon's phone number right away. *Call me—urgent,* was all the message said.

I caught my breath and yelled at Wally, "Wait a minute," and ducked into a pay phone and called her.

When she answered and found it was me, she said, "Oh God, Johnny—come quickly," and hung up.

2

I Smell a Rat

I RAN BACK and into Wally's car and we raced up to Inwood where the little trick house was that they were buying. Naturally, I couldn't answer Wally's hammering questions. She was standing in the crack of the front door as we skidded to a stop in front of the picket fence that boxed their trees and lawn. When I ran through the gate with Wally at my heels, she opened six inches and cried huskily, "Who—who is with you—oh, Wally. Thank God you came too," and as we piled into the gold-and-white front hall, she stood aside, pulling the green silk negligee closer around her shivering little body. Her eyes were glazed and white-ringed.

"In through there—on the terrace," she blurted as she shut the door quickly behind us.

We ran into the green-and-yellow living-room whose French doors opened onto the terrace. Danny lay on the couch in the living-room, his eyes closed, breathing heavily through his mouth. Overcoat and suitcoat were a pile beside him and his collar was open, his battered lumpy face shining wet. There was a half-empty bottle of Scotch and a glass on a coffee table near him and on the floor a pitcher, a sopping wet towel and a spilled bottle of caffeine tablets.

"Why, hell," I said, "he's just drunk. He must of gone on picking up a load looking for Sam. He'll be all...."

"Not him—out there—on the terrace." We hurried on out

to the terrace—and Sam Link.

He wasn't on the terrace but just off it, on the sopping wet ground. His derby hat was beside him. He was on his face, but one crazy staring eye was turned over his shoulder. He was as warm as life but he had no pulse.

Mary's desperate voice blurted: "When I—when Wally brought me home, he made me take a big—a big drink. After he left I went upstairs and tried to read. I must have dozed off. I suddenly heard Sam outside on the lawn—just now—a few minutes ago. It woke me up. He was choking and being ill. Then he started sobbing and threshing around and groaning. I was scared for a minute, till I recognized him. Then I ran down but he was dying when I got to him—convulsions. He's been poisoned, Johnny—hemlock or conine. I know from when I was a nurse—you can smell it—like mice. He—he's been poisoned!"

I knelt there, sick, groggy, trying to get it straight—and then frightened that I *had*.

Wally's quick voice said above me: "When did you find Danny, Mary—before you heard Sam or after?"

"After! I ran out to Sam without noticing Danny was there. I—I didn't see Danny till I ran in to call Johnny."

"Is conine a quick poison?"

"Oh, yes, yes—almost instantaneous."

"Then Sam must have got it within the last—how long? Half hour?"

"No longer."

There was a cold lump in my heart. Danny—with every reason in the world to hate Sam—Danny punched half out of his senses, betrayed by Sam, and blind drunk. Sam killed here within the past few minutes. The obvious story was all there. Cops in books don't care for the obvious, but cops in real life do. The obvious is so damned often all there is. But—poison? I couldn't believe it of Danny.

Wally said: "Mary—get a dollar quick and give it to me."

I sent hot eyes back in through the wide-open terrace doors—and saw the baby rat. I blinked twice, then got half up and plowed in after it, almost banging into Mary as she tried to get in at the same time. The baby rat was under the rosewood piano, near the French doors. It was as stiff as a board, stone dead.

Then I saw the second glass—mate to the one on the coffee table. This one lay on its side, as though it had rolled under the piano. There was a little amber liquid, half dried, lying in it. I smelled the stiffened rat in my hand, then crawled under and smelled the glass. The glass smelled like mice and the rat only vaguely like it. The glass also smelled of liquor.

I CRAWLED OUT as Wally was taking a dollar from Mary's shaking hand and telling her: "All right. Now I'm your lawyer and Danny's. Johnny—get this and get it straight— Danny didn't do this."

I asked eagerly: "How do you know?"

"My God, don't *you* know it?"

I groaned. "What I know won't help. The minute the Homicide Squad sees this and finds Danny was a friend of mine, they'll be after a conviction like hounds."

"I know that."

"And it looks terrible. Mary, can—can you see if that glass under there has that stuff in it? That poison? Don't touch it."

And when, a minute later, she crawled out and stood up and nodded yes, I swallowed. "Then—Sam got his dose right here in this room, less than half an hour ago." My eye fell on the rat. "How the hell do you suppose that beast got...?"

Mary's low voice said: "It's a baby rat. We've been having a pest of them. It wouldn't have enough sense to keep away from the glass and if it got any conine on its nose—the membranes— it would kill it instantly. There's conine in the glass, all right."

I looked miserably at Wally. My voice sounded hollow. "Well, we got to call Homicide." I felt terrible.

The knocker on the front door hammered smartly—and I felt worse.

I grabbed Mary as she started for the hall. "No. You try and get Danny around as fast as you can," and I went out and opened the hall door.

I faced a rail-thin woman, in black to the throat, with a face like an ax. She looked at me out of glittering little black button eyes and rasped eagerly: "Is anything wrong? Is Mr. Harmon all right?"

"What did you think was wrong with him, lady?"

She whipcracked her head in the direction of the living-room. "My window overlooks the terrace out there. I saw Mr. Harmon come in a little while ago and he—well, he was certainly acting queerly. And that other man who was waiting for him out there in the dark..."

"Other...! Wait a minute, lady. Start at the beginning. Exactly what did you see?"

"Why, I saw Mr. Harmon get out of his taxi, about half an hour ago and saw him searching for his keys on the front walk. He was reeling and staggering around. Then he started around toward the side of the house and—and came round to the terrace. While he was fumbling around with the French doors, this other man came out of the darkness behind him and stood in the light on the terrace. He even stood there for a few minutes after Mr. Harmon had gone in, peeking and peering. He started half a dozen times to open the door and go in after him, before he finally did. Then—about ten minutes later—I saw him sort of stumble out again—he was a scrawny little man with a derby hat—and he ducked off into the darkness. I couldn't see what became of him—the trees and everything. And then I saw Mrs. Harmon run out and then run back in— and now you come speeding up here in your car...."

I swallowed and said: "Lady, please think very carefully. Between the time you saw Danny Harmon go in those French doors and the time the man in the derby went in, did you see anyone else out there?"

"Eh? No. Certainly not. There was no one else."

"Did you see any third party around between the time the little guy staggered out and the time Mrs. Harmon came out after him?"

"No. I didn't see anyone else at all. I can assure you that no one crossed that terrace. I was watching very closely."

I said: "Thanks, lady. Who are you?"

"I'm Miss Cartwright—next door."

"We'll investigate. We may call on you later."

WALLY'S EYES WERE hollow, as my lead feet took me back into the living-room. Mary was working on Danny, rubbing his neck desperately and calling his name.

I told Wally, huskily: "Well, you heard it. Danny came in

here alone, twenty minutes ago. Sam was hanging around outside, waiting to see him. He came in right after him. Sam got his dose while he was in here alone with Danny, staggered out and died."

He licked his lips. "Maybe somebody else was already waiting in here. Maybe Danny came in and passed right out. Maybe the other party induced Sam to drink—"

"If there was a third party, he didn't go out the terrace way. There isn't a shred of evidence to show that anyone else was here at all. Unless it was...." I couldn't say it. My sick eyes edged over to Mary's back.

"You fool!" Wally choked. "Mary didn't do it. Nor did Danny."

"I know they didn't—myself. But don't forget—all Homicide will want to know is can they secure a conviction. And it looks awful, Wally."

"Danny had no motive," he persisted desperately. "He didn't realize how Sam had harmed him. His brain is even slower than yours...."

Even that feeble hope went in the next instant.

Danny suddenly moaned, rolled his head feverishly on the couch. The first few words he mumbled were indistinguishable. Then, "... no, no, can't go home... got see Sam... Sam gambled 'way my money... got to see Sam... robbed me...."

I looked at Wally. "What—what the hell is he saying?"

Wally's voice was like tin. "Shut up. Listen. Danny—what makes you think Sam robbed you? That's nonsense."

The kid rolled his battered head. "... know he did... Zimmerman... Zimmie told me... Sam threw our money 'way...."

Mary suddenly cried out falteringly: "Oh, Johnny—he

doesn't mean the money—the half of Danny's purses that Sam was saving for him? Why, that's all we've got."

Wally's face was saffron and lined. He said hoarsely: "Mary—be quiet. Believe me if you never did before—you've got to forget that money. Forget that you knew it was gone—until I told you. And if you want us to have the slightest chance of saving Danny, for God's sake rouse him. Above all, we've got to impress on him not to admit that he knew Sam had tossed away his savings."

I choked: "Wait—you don't mean Sam *did* sink his dough?"

Through tight teeth Wally bit: "Yes, he did. I've no right to divulge a client's business, but the hell with ethics. Sam was...."

Far away the whine of a siren began to rise. Wally whirled his pale face on me and we both stood stiff. Then he snapped: "Get to the phone and notify Homicide, you blockhead. If a prowl car happened to get here before you phone, and *they* notified them, you'd be in the grease. Hurry!"

I groaned at my own blundering, ran out in the hall and made the call. I was holding my breath as the siren drew steadily nearer, praying that it was not coming here. How could...? I swore desperately as I remembered the dumb way I had handled the old maid next door. I had not even shown her my badge.

THEY HAD DANNY sitting up when I plowed back in. Wally had the Kid's face in his hands, rocking his head from side to side. Mary stood aside, the back of one hand pressed to her mouth, her eyes feverish. Wally said: "Danny! Danny! Listen to me: You didn't know Sam had lost that money of yours till I told you. Understand? You've got to blot it out of your memory completely. The cops will be here in a minute. If you admit you knew that, you're done for. You've got to make out you knew nothing about it."

The boy cried out fretfully, sobbingly: *"Did* know 'bout it… dirty crook… fire him manager…."

Wally swung a shining frantic face toward the door as the siren turned into our street. Then he swung back on the kid and his teeth snapped.

"Danny—wake up. You've got to listen. Sam Link is dead, murdered—right outside the door there. If you tell the cops you knew he'd robbed you, they'll think you did it. Do you understand? They'll think you murdered…."

There was just a second while the boy's eyes stayed blank and white-ringed. Then sense came into them. He sprang up, as sober in a half-second as I was, sweat springing out on his face. He grabbed Wally's coat-front, cried out hoarsely: "What? God in Heaven! What did you say? Sam—Sam's dead? Murdered?"

"Yes. And if you admit you knew he'd trimmed you, they'll think you did it. Understand? You've got to forget you knew about it—swear that I told you just now for the first time, that you didn't know it."

The kid's battered face and eyes were frantic and terrified. "But the letter—I told Hymie Annenberg that Sam had gypped me."

"Letter?" Wally exploded hoarsely. "What letter?"

The kid sobbed, clutched his head in his hands. It must have been splitting. His eyes went light, then dark, then light again—half dizzy bewilderment, half scared recollection.

"I—I couldn't find Sam. I looked in dozens of bars. That—

that's how I got drunk. I went up to the office. Zimmerman was there and he—he told me Sam had ruined me—the fight tonight—the money he was keeping for me. He explained everything to me. He—he was cleaning out his desk—quitting. He—he told me I should get a new manager—that Sam was a louse. Hymie Annenberg has been asking me ever since we got to New York. I—I was in a frenzy. I wanted to kill Sam—the money—Mary.... I—I made Zimmerman help me write the letter right there. I—God knows what I said. I was crazy. Then Zimmerman went out with me and helped me mail it."

"Did you say anything about Sam being a crook in it?"

"Yes—yes, I'm sure I did."

"What time did you post it? Think, Danny, for the love of heaven."

The boy made an effort but couldn't answer.

I blurted at Wally: "Who is this Zimmerman? What is it all...?

He flung from the corner of his mouth: "Sam's book-keeper—and his nephew. He's as queer as a three-dollar bill. Danny—are you sure you mailed the letter?"

The whining siren moaned to a stop directly before the house as Danny sobbed: "Yes. Yes. I remember...."

Wally swung his driving hot eyes on me. "It's three o'clock, Johnny. That letter will be delivered some time before ten. The minute Hymie turns it over to Homicide, Danny is sunk. They'll pinch him, take him down and work on him—and they'll have him signing confessions in minutes."

Danny cried out suddenly: "Johnny—Johnny—I didn't kill him, did I?"

My heart turned to water. "No, no, Danny, of course you didn't. Don't you remember?"

"I—I don't remember anything after I sent that letter and went to Ringgold's Bar. I was there—and then suddenly I was here. I thought Sam...."

Heavy knocking sounded on the door. I swung toward it. Wally snatched at my arm and his burning eyes drove into mine. "Johnny—will you go for removing that second glass and that rat under the piano? Then we could claim Sam didn't get it here. I can give them motive for suicide...."

I almost burst with wanting to do it, but I couldn't make it. I swallowed, but I shook my head. I blurted: "I—I can't Wally I'm not smart enough to—figure a thing like that out—carry it off—"

"Then we've got just the next few hours to save Danny's neck. You'll have to do most of it. I'll give them a story that will hold them off, make suicide plausible temporarily—but I'll have to stay right beside the Kid and make sure they don't...."

I swallowed. "Maybe—maybe we can make Hymie Annenberg hold off that letter."

3

The Baron of Homicide

I THANKED GOD fervently a dozen times in the next hour for Wally's swift cool brains, his ability as an actor. When I let the prowl cops in, he was at my heels, but the tenseness was out of his manner and he was like a cucumber.

I said: "Come in, boys. I've notified Homicide."

The cop blinked; "Oh—uh—we didn't know you was here, Johnny."

Wally's voice was lowered and calm. "Just be gentle with the two kids in there, boys. It's a terrible shock to them. Sam Link has committed suicide."

"Suicide? You mean Danny's manager?"

"Yes. He'd lost everything—tossed away all his own holdings and Danny's. He was hopelessly ruined—he explained it to me late this afternoon, though he didn't say he was going to do this. He came out, presumably to tell Danny what had happened, make a clean breast of it before he— I'll explain it all when the Homicide boys get here. The body's outside on the terrace—around the side of the house. It would be a nice gesture if you boys would go around and not disturb the kids any more than you have to."

Instantly, he had them walking on tiptoes. The recorder whispered: "You—the Homicide Squad is coming?"

"Yes. I'll give them the whole story when they do."

He did. He was tops. He pulled my heart back up into its

place and set it ticking again. It had dropped to my boots when I opened the door the second time—to the Homicide circus—and saw that we'd drawn Lieutenant Lebaron. He was the thinnest man on Homicide, very fussy about his clothes, with a face like a skeleton, green eyes and bad teeth. Nobody on the Homicide hated the Broadway Squad any more than Lebaron. They all figure us for grafters and thugs. The Marquis thinks that kind of a rep is good medicine. He builds it up to keep the fear of God in the army of thieves that would like to operate in our section and most of Homicide and, for that matter, the rest of the force believe it literally. Lebaron did. The minute he saw me he stopped dead and his little green eyes flared.

He said: "Johnny Berthold, eh? Well, well. Who have you killed now, you torpedo?"

I tried my best to imitate Wally's cool manner. "Pipe down, stupid. This is no murder, just a suicide. Sam Link, the fight manager knocked himself off because he went bust."

His green eyes sharpened. "Link? Wait a minute. Harmon. This is this Danny Harmon's house? The kid Link sent in to be massacred at the Garden tonight."

"Yeah. Sure. They were like brothers. He come here to say good-bye to Danny, only Danny was too sick and… and… well, Wally Hewlett's here, he was Sam's lawyer and he'll untangle it all for you. Come on." I turned to lead him into the living-room where they were.

He caught my shoulder. "Wait a minute, Johnny. This Danny Harmon is a friend of yours?"

"You're damned tootin'. He…."

I didn't like the sharp light that came in his eyes even then, but he didn't say anything.

We went in where Danny and Mary were sitting on the couch, their arms around each other, looking like two frightened kids. Wally stood, coolly smoking a cigarette, his back to the fireplace.

"I've waited till you got here, Lieutenant, to explain this thing. I want Danny and Mary to hear it, too. They've got to know sooner or later and it might as well be now. Danny—this isn't going to be easy to take, but—well, Sam had gambled away all your money. No, don't interrupt"—the kid had made no move whatever to interrupt—as an actor he was no good at all—"just let me get the whole wretched story off my chest as Sam told it to me this afternoon."

Lebaron said softly: "Wait a minute. Are you trying to tell us that Sam Link, the wise guy that knew all the angles, went broke gambling?"

Wally's face pinched. "Well, he thought he was gambling, Lieutenant. He thought he was playing the cotton market. But he was being played for a sucker. I'm afraid it's the old story of the wisest sharpshooter in his own racket being the biggest sucker for somebody else's. Because he was conned, Lieutenant, neatly and expertly, over a period of four months, for every dime he could raise honestly—and every dime he could 'borrow' *any* way. And that included the cut of Danny's purses that he was holding for the kid. That's what made him feel so bad—that he'd let the kid down. I guess that's why he came here to—to try and explain to Danny before he—did what he did."

"Go on," Lebaron said softly.

Wally looked at the end of his cigarette. "I don't know every last detail of it—only what Sam told me this afternoon. But the only part that bears here is that Sam went overboard, lost his mind or something, and fed this crook every dime he could lay his hands on—and the crook went west, leaving Sam ruined. I don't know just how Sam met him—backstage during rehearsals of some musical show—even Sam couldn't quite remember clearly who introduced them or where. Anyhow, the pup was a smooth worker. He was a distinguished-looking rat—looked like he might have come from some old Boston family—kind of an ascetic face, with wavy black hair and a streak of white right through the middle and a pair of snapping, intelligent blue eyes. I saw him—a couple of times Sam asked me to take envelopes down to him—money, I guess it was—and I can assure you he looked like the McCoy.

"He fed Sam the story that he was secretly working for a big Canadian grain trader who had been ruled off the exchanges. They were supposed to have advance inside news on certain war situations. He had documents, credentials, seals, letterheads—enough to sink a ship, Sam said. He was moaning that he was tired to death of working for this big shot and getting buttons for it, and claimed that, if he only had a little capital, he would be able to make himself a fortune, by taking advantage of the orders he knew were coming up, and so forth.

"Sam went for it, put up several thousand dollars, and the guy bought cotton on margin—or said he did. As you know, cotton has been slowly sagging the last four months and that gave him an excuse to string it out—to milk Sam again and again, urging him to buy more and average up, assuring him that the big rise was imminent and that they could make fortunes.

"The payoff came today. If you gentlemen read the papers, you know that something exploded today in the cotton market.

The price went skyrocketing right after the opening. It is up some two dollars a bale at the close."

WALLY HESITATED, A line on his dark forehead. "Whether this Maples—that's the name he used—actually did know something, actually did have advance notice of this boom, God knows. He could have, but I doubt it. I think it was as much a surprise to him as to anyone. Not that it matters. Maybe he did actually buy cotton with Sam's money, knowing he could cash it in at a moment's notice—it would be legally shrewd as it would make him immune to prosecution as long as he held it. Maybe he doubled the money on the rise today—or maybe not. Maybe he just pocketed Sam's money as it came along, or maybe he actually was in on the big killing today. The fact remains that he melted into thin air when Sam demanded a payoff.

"Sam saw the news this afternoon, just before weighing-in time—two o'clock. He was nearly wild with joy. He'd put himself in a terrible jam to keep feeding money into this merry-go-round. Between ourselves, he'd borrowed from Big Tim Donnelly. Incidentally, I want to get this on the record that I told you this. I represent Big Tim Donnelly also, and I, as his attorney, tell you frankly—Sam had mortgaged everything he owned and—this is the truth as he told it to me tonight— he'd falsified the worth of what he owned to Big Tim, and actually borrowed far more than the value of his security. He'd thrown in Danny's savings. He'd even, in a crazy moment signed for this suicidal match that went on tonight, in order to be able to borrow more quick money. When he read in the papers that the thing had finally come through—that he *had* hit the jackpot, he nearly went out of his head. He phoned this Maples to close him out, and to get everything he had coming, in cash for him, that he would be right down for it.

"I was waiting around his office when he went charging down to Wall Street. And I was there, four hours later when he came back. He went down thinking he was going to get over ninety thousand dollars in cash. He came back with a broken heart. Oh, yes, he had gone through the intermediate stages—shock, fury, frenzy, desperation. But he was too much of a realist not to see through it at last—to see that he had been taken. Evidently this Maples had been ready for flight for weeks. His hotel—the Riordan—where he'd been staying said his bags had been sitting, packed, for that long. Sam's phone call was his signal to run. He destroyed every paper in his office, left nothing in his hotel room, phoned the hotel and had his bags rushed down there, thus leaving no trace—and vanished.

"I tried to get Sam to put you people—the police—on it, but he said it was no use. By then, he realized that Maples was a professional, and a smart one. And once he got that realization through his head, he didn't believe you could do anything that Maples hadn't foreseen—not in time to do any good. You might catch up with him some day, he said, but he had to have the money tonight—that is, last night."

"Why?" Lebaron finally got a chance to snap a word.

Wally shrugged. "He didn't tell me that."

LEBARON'S GLITTERING LITTLE green eyes went over to Mary and Danny. "When did you find out he'd clipped *you?* Did you put the pressure on him to get it up tonight, maybe?"

Mary's soft little face was desperate, her pansy eyes almost black. "No, no—we just heard it now—for the first time. We didn't know...."

"You!" Lebaron shot at Danny.

Danny's voice was thick and hoarse as he echoed: "No. We— We just found out now."

I tightened up inside. We were out on a limb now. Danny had told his first lie. The whole dangerous business was hardening up. I had to—we had to—get things set once and for all before that cursed letter reached Hymie Annenberg.

Hymie Annenberg! Sweat broke out all over me. I mumbled something about being right back and hastily edged my way to the door.

On the way out, I heard Lebaron ask Danny sharply: "What's the matter with you? Are you drunk?"

Wally's voice replied smoothly: "He's not so much drunk as ill and bone-weary from the beating—the fight tonight. I induced him to take a drink or two to relax him."

I hurried out, spotted a drug store on the corner and made a bee-line for the phone booth. My watch said eight minutes to four. I estimated that my boss, the Marquis, would about be at Benny's Bar and Grill by now and I called there and he was.

I threw at him: "Boss—can you get Hymie Annenberg to do you a favor?

He said: "No."

I sweated. I said: "Well, you gotta, chief. It's—well, a friend of mine may be facing a murder rap if you don't." His "What?" nearly took my ear off. Then, "I couldn't get the time of day from Hymie Annenberg, and I wouldn't want it. He's a chiseling little conniver and he knows I'd stick one in him any time.

What's this about murder?"

I told him.

When he got through swearing, he asked: "What did I tell you, you damned blockhead?"

"Not—never to try and handle a murder case alone, chief, I know—but what could I do? And—and I'm not exactly handling it alone."

"Tell it to me over again. Every damned last detail."

I did and then he said, "Once more," and I sweated through that.

I thought he had left the phone. My nickel tumbled down and I said, "Boss, boss," and dug for another.

"I'm here, you ape. Did you say Big Tim Donnelly was betting on a knockout tonight?"

"Yeah. But boss—that letter to Hymie—"

"Nothing can be done about it. Trying to stop that will only get us all facing accomplice charges. Damn you, why do you have to pick this time to tangle in a killing. I'm tied up here for an hour and a half. What did you say that book-keeper's name was—the one that seems to have been helping Danny write letters?"

"Zimmerman. Hey—you don't think—listen, boss—could you have McGuire or one of the squad grab that Zimmerman and bring him up here?"

"And have him inform Lebaron that Danny knew all about the money situation last night? Very bright. Listen—you sit tight and try not get into any jams till I get through here. Call me in and hour and a half at MacCreagh's Ticket Agency."

He hung up.

I GUESS THAT was the lowest point of the night for me. I was floundering. I thought the boss had brushed me off and I began to get a little panicky. Maybe I hadn't explained to him how fond I was of Danny and—well, Mary. Maybe I....

That book-keeper! It suddenly seemed that he might be a regular mine of evidence. Information, anyway. Or anyway he ought to be talked to. And I had done just about as much standing around as I could. Danny and Mary were in the best possible hands. Anything that cropped up at the house would be taken care of. And somebody had to pile out and dig up something. Who, if not me?

Or maybe it was that I just didn't want to go back to the house where Sam Link lay, didn't want to be around when the crafty Lebaron was popping questions, didn't want to see Danny and Mary going through the mill—and didn't want to chance putting my big foot in it myself. Anyway, I beat it for the subway when I left the drug store and rode down to Broadway.

I don't know why I didn't start wondering where he lived before I rode down. I had some idea that he might be in the phone book but he wasn't and I shied away from calling back to the house and trying to get it out of Wally, what with Lebaron and the others right around him. I was near Sam's office when I got off the subway and I sort of wandered over toward it. No, I wasn't dumb enough to think he might be there. If you got to know, I was wondering if I couldn't ease my way into the place and pick up his address somewhere around.

That idea was chased out of my head when I strolled round onto Eighth Avenue, and was in front of Sam's office building.

Big Tim Donnelly was standing in the gutter, staring sourly

up at the lighted second-floor offices. His heavy black eyebrows were a straight bar across his big red face.

All of a sudden I started thinking. Big Tim had been in the booze-and-boat business during prohibition—putting the booze into boats and taking it places. He was supposed to have taken a half million dollars out of that. Since repeal, he had got a lot more legal, bought a professional hockey club, some race horses, a string of taverns and some Coney Island concessions, but he had been as deadly as they come not long ago, and if Sam Link had clipped him for some money....

I said: "Hey, what are you looking for?"

"Sam Link. What's it to you, copper?"

"It might be a poke in the mush to you, if you don't watch your lip. Sam Link's dead and I got a damned good hunch you know it."

He stared at me dumbly for a good minute.

"All right," I yapped impatiently. "Come clean. You knocked him off, eh?"

He took a long breath and his ice-gray eyes were heavy. After a minute he said softly: "Coppers don't talk to me like that, Johnny. Not no more. I'm a businessman and a taxpayer and I got some mighty good friends down at City Hall."

"I'll knock you all the way into their laps if you try that guff with me," I pointed out. "Get this—and get it straight. Sam is dead and the kid they're trying to pin it on is a friend of mine. I've got till morning to crack it and I'm not worried much right now about anybody's wires. Sam Link owed you money—phonied you to get it out of you. But you gave him a chance, didn't you—even after you found he'd pulled a fast one?"

"Take it easy, Johnny. That idea isn't the kind you can handle."

"This one is. In fact, it looks better every time I go over it. Sam owed you dough—the hard way. You gave him till tonight to get it up. Up till three o'clock today he didn't think he could get it up—and after seven, he knew he couldn't. But you gave him an out. You told him you'd write it off, if Danny Harmon was knocked out. You must have thought it was in the bag, because I hear you dropped plenty betting that way. Naturally, when even that fell down on you, you went after Sam and caught up to him up at Danny Harmon's place and gave him the business."

I DON'T KNOW who was most surprised when I rolled that out—Tim or me. But it was reasonable—reasonable as hell.

But that didn't mean you couldn't have knocked me over with a feather when he practically admitted it by saying: "That crooked little —— four-eyed book-keeper told you that, didn't he?"

I said, "Uh—"

"You're a liar. He did. I've noticed the little pansy sneaking around, hiding behind doors, trying to get an earful every time I've been in to see Sam. How do you know Sam was knocked off? How do you know he didn't do the Dutch? The louse was singing the blues plenty tonight."

"I know."

"What about that pug of his—Danny Harmon? If ever a guy got a dirty deal, Harmon did. Maybe he got enough sense in *his* thick head—"

"Danny Harmon didn't do it."

"Then the four-eyes did. Don't waste your time putting it on me. I haven't touched a gun in six years and I'm strictly legitimate. Besides, I got an alibi."

"Why would Zimmerman do it?"

"How do I know? He's a sneaky little rat and he's probably got an angle somewhere. Anyway, he's Sam's nephew and I suppose he inherits anything there is to inherit. As for me—all right, I told Sam I was betting on a knockout and if it came off, we'd call it square, but he gave me no nod. It was my own judgment I was backing. If I had got his O.K. on it, I'd of give him a clean bill anyway the way it turned out. He *tried* to toss in the diaper, didn't he?"

I knew there was something wrong in his story, but I couldn't put my finger on it. And then I did.

"Hey, wait a minute. How do you know you got an alibi if you didn't know he was dead? How do you know what time he got it?"

"——— ——— all smart coppers," he said in a tired voice. He took my arm and turned me around, pointed out a Lincoln sedan parked across the road. I could see vague forms in it. "Look, Hawkshaw. There's three guys in there. One of them is on the City Council. I been with them ever since the fight—in fact they sat with me during the fight. We were heading down to the Village and passed here and saw a light and I came over to see if maybe Sam was up in his office. He isn't. Nobody is. Somebody just left the lights on, I guess. Now I'm on my way—or do you want to make a pinch? One way or the other?" And when I couldn't decide, he patted the air and turned away. "Get that fluffy-haired little four-eyed rat. He's your meat—somehow. Take my word for it."

"How could I find him? Wait a minute. What the hell's your rush?" I growled.

"Chum, dead or alive, Sam Link owes me plenty of grands. I'm going to try and make sure I collect what I can. That Zimmerman lives in the Hotel Premier, I think. S'long."

FROM WHERE I stood, I could see the Premier's red neon sign over the building tops, two blocks west. I hurried over there—only to have the fancy-looking clerk tell me: "I'm sorry, he doesn't answer. I believe you'll find him still at his office. He said he might be there very late."

I bawled, "At this hour?" and then looked up at the clock.

It damned near floored me. I went cold all over. It was twenty minutes to six. A whole hour and a half had dropped away from under me, and I—

I remembered that I was supposed to call the Marquis at five thirty and I dived into a phone booth. I rang the Agency and the phone barely gave a tinkle before his soft voice answered quickly: "Well? Where the hell have you been? Have they got anywhere yet?"

I somehow didn't like to tell him I was way downtown. "N-no. I've been out of the house for a few minutes. Up till I left, they were still hammering at Danny."

"Listen—are you positive Danny *didn't* do it?"

"God Almighty, yes, chief. Forget that."

"God help you if you're wrong. I've got to know before I go ahead with this."

I blurted: "The only way we can go ahead with it now is to stop that letter. Hell, for all I know, it may catch an early delivery and be there in an hour. If you could have started before—"

His voice snarled: "Because I couldn't do it myself, doesn't mean it wasn't done. I happen to have twenty-two men working for me, you stupe. Two thirds of the Squad have been racing round town on your problem."

I almost bawled: "Judas—you mean the boys...?"

"Shut up. We've got something that may pan out, or may not. Get to hell back to the house. Then call me and tell me if anything new's happened. And then listen carefully to what I say. And—now get this—above all, don't let anybody know that you're not working strictly alone. If you break this, you break it alone. That pup Lebaron has to be taught that the dumbest lug on my squad is still smarter than he is. Now, move!"

I realized how long it took on the subway, this time—because I was on fire again, not bogged down with thinking. The boss had something—or at least was working on it! Hope was jumping up and down in my noodle.

ALMOST ALL THE flock of cars that had been around the house were gone now. Only three or four remained. There was still a thin crowd as I hurried up the walk. The Homicide dick on the door said dully, as he passed me in: "We thought we were rid of you."

I mumbled something and started for the living-room. I stopped dead as I looked through the doorway—and saw Big Tim Donnelly standing there glowering. It seemed like a magic trick— I had just left him downtown and here he was uptown. Homicide must have been after him even while I was, and picked him up the minute he left me.

Inside the living-room a fretful, peevish little falsetto voice was saying: "Of course I told Danny what had happened—this evening—or if you prefer, last evening, when he came into the office looking for Mr. Link."

"Why did you take it on yourself to tell him? And why urge him to write that letter to Hymie Annenberg, asking him to be his new manager?"

I went cold. I might have known Lebaron was too smart to be stalled off. We were sunk.

The peevish soprano went on. "Because I thought it perfectly wretched that he—that such a magnificent specimen of young manhood should be victimized by my uncle. I was raging."

My head buzzed. I almost stumbled to the door of the room, looked in just long enough to see the be-spectacled little runt standing with his hands on his hips. He had reddish snuff-colored powdery hair, gray-sprinkled, a round, red-cheeked face and I swear he wore lipstick. His eyes were purple-blue behind the thick lenses. He looked round at me with a flash of annoyance, then dismissed me.

Lebaron got up from where he had been sitting and looked down at Danny and Mary. Beyond them, I could see Wally's pale, hunted face as he gave me a desperate questioning look and wiped his damp face.

"So," Lebaron's soft voice said. "You were blind drunk last night—sore enough at Sam Link to do a crazy thing like that. You knew all the answers by the time he came here to see you. Yet you lied to me—told me you didn't."

Wally said sharply, desperately: "We still maintain that Danny was drunk and doesn't remember it. Mr. Zimmerman here confirms that."

"Yeah. Well—I'm taking him in—" Then Lebaron's green eyes fell on me for the first time and he jerked around. "You, eh? I thought you'd realized you were out of your depth and taken a powder."

I damned near said things I shouldn't, he made me so mad. But I knew one mistake now would be too much. So I choked it all down but a, "Yeah? You were wrong."

I HURRIED OUT to the phone, called the Marquis and, holding my hands cupped over the mouthpiece, blurted the whole thing at him.

He raged: "I ought to drop you to stew in your own grease. Who told you to go chasing—well, never mind. Get everything out of your head except what I'm going to tell you now. Ready?

"I want you to repeat what I say. Repeat it loud enough so that anybody in the other room or anywhere else that is trying to listen in, can. Got that? All right. First say 'All right. Let me speak to the hacker.'"

I gulped, took my hands away from my mouth and said: "Let me speak to the hacker."

"Now say"—well, this is what he said and I repeated it word for word: "Hello, hacker? You got something for me?... Where? Mell Street... What?... Number Fifty-four... Yeah. Yeah. I got that... Nordon Corporation... Yeah, all right... Yeah, I'll take care of you plenty."

When we had got that off, the Marquis warned me not to continue broadcasting, and told me: "As soon as you leave the phone, hang around just a minute or two, look wise, and then beat it down to Fifty-four Mell Street. It's a block of empty stores down by the waterfront. They're all separate stores, but they have a common loft. Go to the one on the very west end. Got that? The west end one. The door will be open. Go in, climb up to the loft and belly your way to the other end of the building. There's a hot air register there—that looks down into the room I want you to watch."

I said: "Wait, wait—let me have that again."

I drove it into my brain as he repeated it slowly. "O.K.—and then?"

"Then pray to God that things happen—and try to use your judgment. Now remember—you're working alone on this thing. You haven't even contacted me. If Lebaron asks you any questions—or anybody else, even Danny or Mary—*anybody*—just look wise and say you're hot but you can't spill one word yet. Remember—you're a mastermind now!"

I got up from the phone to find the whole crowd standing in the doorway watching me. Lebaron was holding the hiccuping Danny by the hand and Mary was clinging to him, tears streaming down her face. Wally's eyes were desperately questioning me, even as he snatched for his hat and snapped at Lebaron: "Where will you take him? To headquarters?"

"Yeah. To headquarters."

I gave Wally a little reassuring nod and said to Lebaron: "Try and keep him there. Just try, stupid."

I saw Big Tim Donnelly's cold gray eyes frowning at me muddily. And I saw the grape-blue, swollen-looking ones of the book-keeper, Zimmerman, search me with little pin-points of light far back in them.

I strode out the door, not even saying a word to Danny and Mary. I couldn't. The stunned, sick fear on their faces had me nearly crazy as it was. Words couldn't have helped it. Nothing could help it—unless this crazy-sounding thing of the Marquis came through.

Wally ran down the steps after me, pleading: "For God's sake, Johnny—have you got anything? That devil Lebaron—"

"Don't worry. Just hold your hat," I said. "We've still got an hour—and it may be enough."

"God, I hope so. I'm beating it down to Judge Rodgers to get a writ. If you can dig up anything by morning—I'm terrified at what that kid'll say or sign if they get working on him—"

"Don't worry. That's all. Don't worry," I said, and left him.

All the way down to Mell Street in a cab I kept going over it in my mind to make sure I had everything right.

HONEST, I NEVER saw anything look so dead. The four stores—it was a corner building—were all empty. Torn paper and orphan pieces of furniture loomed vaguely through the dirty windows as I slipped by in the shadows on the other side. Wind blew in like knives from the lashing ocean, beyond the ferry slips. Nowhere did anything move or make sound in the black wet night. Vaguely I could see signs propped drunkenly in the windows—something about remodeling building to suit—with the block letters of the Nordon Corporation underneath. Evidently they owned the gloomy structure.

I was almost surprised to find the end door open. I half expected that they had all been nailed shut for years. I groped my way into a dank, bitter cold store, filthy with debris and broken furniture. The ceiling was high, old-fashioned. Vaguely I could see a door standing open in the rear wall. I picked my way to it and was in a second, larger room at the back of the store. Mostly old packing cases and wrappers were here.

There was a ladder to a trapdoor in one corner.

If the downstairs had been cold, the upstairs was an icebox. The loft was shallow, just barely high enough for me to crouch over and move along. I gave one spurt of my flash before I started, got the general layout of the beams ahead of me—and spotted the line of hot air registers. They were along the ceilings of the back rooms of the stores. I didn't know if I was supposed to be so careful or not, but I swear I didn't even let a board creak by the time I was flat on my belly, staring down through the register-grill into the box-littered room below.

I don't know how long I waited, straining my eyes, totally unable to see anything except the vague lumpy forms of boxes. To me it seemed hours. Nothing happened. Nothing moved. My heart began to hammer, as minute after minute dropped away. The whole thing was a wash-out. Nothing was going to happen.

Then it went off.

The first faintly scraping footstep in the alley behind the store, almost made me jump, my nerves were screwed up so by the time it came. I glued my face to the ice-cold register. I heard a key slip softly into a lock, heard it turn, heard someone ease quickly in and close the door behind them. I knew he was in the room below me, but I could not see him.

Then he turned a flashlight on—and I could.

Big Tim Donnelly was in the litter beneath me, poking his flashlight around, searching for something.

He found something. I damned near yelled. His torch-beam swung round finally to the rear corner of the room— and picked out the Marquis. The Chief was sitting casually in a broken chair, one leg of which he had propped up with a box. His dapper little body was at ease, his knees crossed, his small, black gloved hands loosely clasped in front of him, his thumbs twiddling. His little pink-cheeked Santa Claus face was placid, his deep-set China blue eyes politely interested under his hard hat.

He said: "Oh, hello, Tim."

The gasping Donnelly had practically jumped backwards toward the front of the room and I could no longer see him. His voice was tense and harsh.

"What the hell are you doing here?"

"I thought cops were supposed to ask the questions. What are you?"

"I own this joint. I heard that lamebrain of yours mention this building and I wouldn't put it past him to try and frame me."

"You're the Nordon Corporation?"

"Yeah. I had a partner once named Norris and we made the label up out of our names. What the hell's going on here?"

Then for the first time he—and I—saw the two oversize pigskin bags sitting in the corner. His jaw sagged. "What—hey what—are those yours?"

"No chum. Those are the belongings of the late Mr. Maples."

"Map—*late*—hey, what the—you mean—is that the guy Maples that took Sam Link for my dough?"

"Well, that's what we're trying to find out," the Marquis said softly. "Whether he took Sam for your dough, I mean—not whether the bags are Maples'. They are."

"Well—well who brought them here?"

"Mr. Maples did."

THERE WAS A silence, while Donnelly's heavy breathing puffed out steam into the beam of the flash. "Well, where is he? What's the idea?" He gave a short bark. "Ha! If this is the best he can afford in the way of rooms, he's welcome."

"I think he's enjoying it, as well as he would any other place," the Marquis said.

"Well, why—*what? What was that you said? He....*"

The Marquis nodded at a sagging, tall box against the wall near him. "This is not exactly a cupboard, rather the box that once contained a cupboard. Nevertheless, it opens the way a cupboard does. If you'll just undo that hasp-and-nail, Tim, we'll...."

Donnelly made a quick stride and yanked. The door swayed slowly open.

The man inside had slid down—or been pushed down—till his knees were opposite his face. His face leaned against them peeking out. He was—or had been—a fine-looking man. His glazed brown eyes still had a trace of fire and snap to them. His wavy brown hair had a white streak, straight through the middle of it, and some of the blood from the smashed mess that was his right temple had smeared the streak. He had been dead some hours.

Donnelly stumbled backwards. "Jumping hell! What is this—a frame?"

"I don't think so. The way it looks to me, Tim, is that somebody—just for the sake of argument let's say you—was very much interested in Sam Link's financial affairs. You—knowing how much dough he was laying out from time to time—would be in a good spot to get curious. Say you snooped around. Say you found out he was being taken—and say you decided to run a racket-within a racket, as it were. Or, in other words—words that you will recall better—a little hi-jacking.

"Now suppose you kept in close touch—suppose you even had some one working for you, tipping you off to every move Sam made—anyhow finding out somehow. Then came the blow-off today when you knew this Maples would have to either get a fortune up—or duck out. Knowing he'd been keeping his bags poised for a getaway in his hotel, you figured he'd probably duck. Moreover Sam phoned him at two o'clock and told him to get *his*—Sam's—funds all in cash. So that removed any doubt. Whether Maples was planning to run or pay, he was certain to have a lush sum in cold cash in his office. So you beat it down there.

"Maybe you stalled around till he put the cash where you could see it. But you must have worked fast—because there wasn't much time to do what was done. I refer, of course, to your putting a gun on Maples, forcing him to call and have his bags delivered there from the hotel, and—managing somehow to get him down here to these empty stores where you could do him in. I say managing, because the taxi driver who brought him here—oh, yes, that's how we got on to the business—by locating the hacker—the taxi driver swears he came here alone. My guess is you took *all* the money, but promised him his share if he came here to get it—maybe with some gag that he could only have it if he jumped a boat—I don't know. Anyway, you got him here and killed him, after, of course, cleaning out his office so that it was empty when Sam Link reached there.

"But Sam Link isn't a fool and anybody with half a brain knows that he wouldn't fall for anything as phony as this would prove to be once he put his nose to it. The only safe way was to kill Sam—and for upwards of a hundred thousand dollars it was worth it, eh? So Sam had to go, because he was too smart and might get to thinking."

BIG TIM DONNELLY'S breath was harsh and fast. He

said hoarsely: "You can't prove a thing on me—not any part of that. I have an alibi for all afternoon and all evening. I was in the company of several people both at the time this guy got it and the time Sam was poisoned—"

"You always were pretty good on the alibis, Tim. But you can relax. I was running off at the mouth. You didn't kill them—either of them. I was just kidding."

"Kidding? A hell of a way to kid. Who did kill them?"

"Who? Why the little rat whom Johnny frightened to death by mentioning this address—the little rat that just slid in through the door behind you while I was talking, the little rat that...."

Donnelly tried to whirl, but the shrill, falsetto voice behind him squealed: "Drop that light—drop it—turn it off—I'll shoot...."

Donnelly gasped and the light went dark in his hand. A second, thinner, more piercing one sprang alight behind him and the muzzle of a gun was just visible underneath it. The peevish, womanish voice cried hastily: "Don't move—either of you. I'll shoot—I surely will."

Donnelly's big face was stupid and incredulous. "Zimmerman? By God!"

"Silence!"

Up in the loft, I was thunderstruck. Like a fool, I had been watching the Marquis with my mouth open, while he talked. I had not seen nor heard the little killer come in. He must have moved without sound to catch Big Tim flat-footed.

He said in his peevish soprano: "You—both of you—go out and lie down on the floor—put your hands high above your heads—quickly!"

The Marquis' lazy voice said: "What if we don't, life-taker? Even for a hundred thousand dollars, you aren't going to start butchering your way out like this. You aren't going to kill us—and then Johnny when he gets here—and then anybody else he may have popped off to—and then—"

"Stop it!" The other's shrill was almost a scream. "I—I'm not going to kill anybody—if I can help it. I—I don't know what I'll do! But you shan't capture me alive—I swear it. Lie down there so that I may search you, both of you!"

For another minute, I thought the Marquis was going to refuse. I lay there, my eyes bulging. The Marquis slowly got to his feet, walked over, knelt down and went down on his face. Big Tim growled in his throat, but he did likewise.

I wondered if the Marquis was really going to let himself be frisked. I thought to myself it would be a hell of a gag—I could blackmail him from now on about this if he did.

I nearly went out of my head as I saw what happened the next instant.

The Marquis drawled as he went down: "Yes, come to think of it—you *were* the one in the ideal position to swing it, weren't you. And of course that dead rat was the giveaway. I bet you went nearly nuts when you saw it."

I heard the sharp intake of breath from behind the light—and then something flashed. The little killer said suddenly, in a voice that was nothing at all like the pansy Zimmerman which he had been aping, "Damn you, Marquis—so you *did* get it," and plunged forward, a long-bladed knife sweeping upward in his hand. "It won't do...."

I got my scrambled brains together and fired through the grating then. But my aim was hasty. I got him in the foot, however, and it kicked out from under him, dropped him short of the Marquis. He shouted a curse, whirled and fired up at me—and the whole grating of the register seemed to slap me in the puss. My face went numb as I tried to fire again. But the Marquis had rolled over like lightning and the short belly gun that he had gotten from his clothes in the furor hammered twice and the gun went flying out of the murderer's hand and he pitched down, grabbing at his chest, howling once.

The Marquis' gun was already out of sight when I fingered the button of my powerful torch and flooded the grimy room below with cross-barred light. Before I could say anything, he yelped up at me: "Nice going, Johnny. For a minute there, I thought you'd lost control of the situation, but I didn't realize how smart you were. Come on down. Well, Wally—how do you like dying?"

I was halfway to my feet when he said that and I nearly fell down flat again. "Wally—did you say—my God, is that killer Wally?"

The Marquis laughed hastily. "I don't know who else you expected. You told me you knew hours ago that it was Wally—because of the dead rat."

I started to shout: "What?" before sense hammered back into my noodle— the recollection that I was supposed to be a mastermind here. I beat it downstairs and came out into the room just as the Marquis asked: "Well, mouthpiece? If only you'd moved a little faster to get this body out of here—or if Johnny didn't happen to notice that that dead rat was stiff— meaning that it had been dead over two hours—you would have been sitting pretty, eh?"

Wally was propped up on one elbow, his dark, fine-looking

face dingy and drawn. His black eyes examined me curiously. He might have been resting, taking a sun bath on some beach except for the blood that was pouring out, soaking his clothes.

He said slowly: "If Johnny figured that out, I deserved to die. I had him pegged as dumb."

"Ha-ha!" I said hollowly. "That's a hot one."

SIRENS WERE ALREADY beginning to sound off— brought by the shooting. I grabbed the Marquis and got him in the front room. "For God's sake," I begged. "What's this about the dead rat? I don't get it."

"It's little enough—but it's supposed to be the start of your masterminding. The rat had been dead two hours—had to be board-stiff as you found him—from poison in the glass that was supposed to have fallen there only a few minutes before. That meant the glass had been there a long time—long before Sam died. Wally was the logical one to have put it there—when he took Mary home. He wouldn't have put it there if he hadn't known he was going to kill Sam with that poison. The idea was that, *wherever* Sam dropped, that glass would be found in Danny's place and tie the Kid to it. It was pure luck that the little weasel elected to go to see Danny, just about when his time was up, wasn't it?"

"Time was up?" I almost yelled. "My God, Marty—didn't I tell you Wally was with me every minute from fight time till the time we were called to Mary's—"

"Yes, yes. But that isn't hard. When we find out where Wally got the conine—it's a rare poison and now that he's nabbed we can find the crooked doctor or pharmacist who sold it to him easily enough—and also find how he got it into Sam. My guess—or your guess—is that he got an extra-thick capsule—one that wouldn't dissolve in the stomach for an hour or two—and put it in with Sam's stomach capsules. Sam took it when Wally wasn't even around, carried it around till it dissolved—and then died while Wally had a complete alibi with you. And then the pup has the nerve to declare himself in on the investigation so as to be on hand to boggle up everything that looked like it might point to him. Now get that into your head, and remember—you solved this. I was just giving you a hand with the trap here."

He listened a minute to the now screaming sirens outside the door. His teeth snapped and he half whispered: "Later—I want to see you in my apartment. And bring your sap. I'm going to bend it over your head."

Then the first of the prowl cops poured in and the Marquis led them back to where Wally was sleeping peacefully, Donnelly sitting gloomily on a bale, watching him die.

My head still aches from the lumps the chief gave me, but the startled, grateful look in Mary's wet eyes when we went and got Danny out of the can and took him home, would have paid for it a dozen times over.

The black fury and consternation on Lebaron's skeleton puss was pure gravy.

Murder Done in Gold

Ace McGuire—straw-bossing the Broadway Squad in the Marquis' absence—was praying the lid would stay tight on the Tenderloin till his lieutenant returned. Then—BROADWAY GAMBLER SLAIN! screamed the headlines. So Ace had to nab the killer because he knew damn well the Marquis—just back from a fishing trip—wouldn't want to hear about "the big one that got away."

1

The Lid Blows Off

THE GIRL GOT out of the taxi on Fifty-eighth, maybe
sixty feet from me along toward Seventh Avenue. The cab
rattled away, left her standing there snapping shut her black
bag in her dark-gloved hands.

She had on black satin. All I could see was her back, of
course, but it was a sweet back, trim and smooth, tapering with
exactly the right curves down to trim, artistic legs. Her hair was
a shining black doughnut low on her neck, her hat a splash of
black on the side of her head spouting a long thin red feather.
I gave it, along with the rest of her, my silent approval.

She kept on standing there evidently watching something
down the street. Presently I craned my neck to see what it
was but I couldn't locate anything except a shirt-sleeved giant
midway down the block who popped up from an apartment
house areaway spasmodically, wrestling ash-barrels. Nothing
else moved on the dark street.

Presently it became apparent that the giant sure enough, was
what she was watching. He vanished down into his areaway
and she hurried along. There was no rattle of heels, so I divined
she was walking carefully on her toes. When he reappeared
again, she swayed quickly over close to the building fronts and
stopped.

I decided, after consideration, that it was all right with
me, whatever the game was. I was just resting my shoulders

against the corner building and relaxing a few minutes. I had made the one o'clock round of the section, and I was feeling good. There were exactly three more days before my boss, the Marquis—Lieutenant Marquis to you, kingpin of the Squad *and* of Broadway too, in case you're in any doubt—was due back from his spring fishing trip. I had started out straw-bossing the district with my heart in my throat, but in fourteen days, my fervent prayers had got results. The lid was on tight. There's always felony on Broadway, but the kind that does us serious damage—there hadn't been a breath of it. It looked as though everything was all right.

And then suddenly everything was all wrong—at least under my eyes. The girl threw a quick, nervous glance back toward my corner and I recognized her as Dixie Higgins.

I CAME UP off my back as though something had stung me. Dixie Higgins had been bodily thrown out of the district by the Marquis himself eight months ago and categorically warned never to set so much as a foot here again. She was a beautiful girl, with lily-white skin, slender streamlined figure and granite-blue eyes—and she was pure thermite. Stealing was a gnawing disease with her, either scheming for thousands or lush-rolling for dimes. She might have been an important thief if she hadn't been man-crazy on the side. Put that combination in a package like hers and set it on Broadway and you *know* you have a fire bomb—one that never stops going off. I was down the street after her the minute I tagged her.

But I was a step behind and I was good and mad. Hell, when the Marquis warns them off the Street, the biggest thieves in the world take it. We—twenty-two of us—couldn't boss

Titanic stood there—a nail brush in one hand, the girl's fingers in the other.

Broadway for an hour if we didn't back *that*. And this damned little tart....

The giant janitor was invisible again and she was speeding toward the arched door of his gray cut-stone trim little apartment house. I yelled "Hey!" and whistled at her. "Hey—*you!*"

She gave me one hasty backward look—and then ran the last ten steps and darted through the street-level glass door of the apartment house. That made me madder. I went after her. When I slid to a stop and snatched at the door myself, I could still see her, running away down the long narrow hall—the apartment house was deeper than it looked from outside, had stairs at the left and a long lighted hall that ran to a back door on the right. Her silken legs flashed out the back door as I whipped open the front.

The shirt-sleeved giant—a County Cardiff bogtrotter with hair as red as mine and a cheap-rye breath that preceded him for yards—swung leisurely out of the basement stairs squarely in my path. He saw me charging toward him and, half-tanked as he was, hastily planted himself, scowled me over quickly, jabbed out a hand like a bread board. "Hey, wa-iddd a minute! Waiiiiid—" he decided.

Somewhere behind the back door there was sound. It was like someone pounding the lid of a closed grand piano with a lead pipe four times. One. Two-three. Four.

I slapped his hand aside, snarled: "Get out of my way, you lunkhead. I want that girl—"

I don't know how he threw the punch that quick—a short whistling hook from behind his back. He must have had it ready. It wasn't a hard punch but it slammed me off balance against the side of the wall, and his drunken crafty eyes darkened as he fell after me. "Girl, eh?" he panted. "You ——!"

I gave him the flat of my gun on his jawbone, just as hard as whipping it out of my shoulder clip and slashing would permit and he went sailing backwards, wailing, his hands over his face. I didn't realize that he had fallen over the banister till I heard the crash as I snatched open the back door and I didn't care a damn if he had broken his neck.

I tucked the gun away and plunged out into a little garden—

cement-paved but still a garden. There was a trim little two-story square house of the same gray stone facing me. It had window boxes with flowers, and two little white sandstone steps up to the front door, with white sandstone balustrades. There was one tree in the yard—over against the board fence at the left. The door was open a crack and I started for it. A dark, low shadow inside the lighted crack became a man picking something up. He almost tripped on his own hand as he tried to grab it, straighten up, and step out onto the little stoop simultaneously. Then he stopped, rocked a little on his heels as he saw me coming, turtled his neck to peer at me and brought up the gun in his hand.

I guess light fell on my red hair and freckles because he relaxed the gun and grumbled sneeringly: "Oh, it's Mickey himself McGuire. Tie that." And as I stopped, he lounged deliberately over against the white sandstone balustrade. "Well, what do *you* want, copper?"

He was Tommy Content, a youthful gambler who had been on the Street for only a few months, but whose savvy and honesty had surprisingly gotten the Marquis' O.K. From his thick tones, *he* was drunk, too, and he hadn't yet gotten over a bitter sort of cop-hating that he had brought from the west.

"The girl, Tommy," I said. I was in no rush now. I had chased her up an alley. I could see through the open door of the house behind him and I recognized the type—a studio with no bolt-hole. One enormous skylighted room with maybe a little balcony for a bedroom and bathroom—but no back door. "Get her out here. And my name's Ace, not Mickey, if you like your own teeth."

HE DELIBERATELY SETTLED himself in a more slovenly lounge on the low balustrade and spat. He had a narrow, dark face with a movie-idol profile and queer mahogany hair that was like a too-big frizzly wig parted in the middle. He usually wore glasses but he hadn't them on now and he had to squint down at me. "Girl?" he mocked, thick-tongued. "What girl? No girl here, Mickey."

"Can it," I warned him. "The Marquis gave that babe a floater and you'll get the same if you front—"

He blurted suddenly in a crazy wailing sob: "I told you there was no jane here!"

I blew out breath, took the gun out of my clip again. "All right, chump. I don't like squabbling with drunks, but I can. Drop that iron if you don't want trouble."

He mouthed a queer indrawn sob—and then the madness exploded. He moaned, "Trouble, ha-ha," and threw me the spectacles in his hand. At least that was what I thought he was doing. They landed fairly in my palm, I looked down startled— and then he plunged suddenly into my arms, as limp as a rag doll. I had to jerk my face away in disgust from his sweat-turgid one and he breathed heavily on my neck as I staggered, stuffing the spectacles in my pocket, trying to support him.

I raged: "You drunken ——! Get off—"

The door of the apartment house behind me closed sharply and I whipped my head around—to hear high heels race away down the hall inside. I was wild with fury. I hefted him viciously to get my palms against his shoulders and heave him off me—and my eye fell on the balustrade.

He slid down my front as I congealed. I just kicked out a foot in time to keep his face from cracking on the bare cement. I was frozen in my tracks. Long, thin, dark figures of irregular length had run down the white sandstone of the balustrade against which he had been leaning. I whipped out my flashlight from my pocket, squirted light—and the streamers were dark ugly red. I gasped, flung the light beam down to him at my feet—and my hackles rose. He was half on his face, half on his left side. His right arm was away from his body and there were four soggy, ragged dark holes in his brown suit, up and down between armpit and belt-line.

I choked, "God Almighty," whirled and jumped for the apartment house—then checked and danced back in crazy indecision, finally threw myself in pursuit of the girl like a madman, tore down the hall and dived out onto Fifty-eighth—and faced a dark, quiet street, with not a breath of sound anywhere.

My head was pounding. This was it! This was the explosion that I had been praying tormentedly against. For I hadn't the slightest doubt that the gambler inside was going to die. He was torn to pieces internally—must be. There was almost a touch of panic in my heart as I ran feverishly around, trying to spot her if she were hiding nearby.

If she was, I couldn't find her—and the man was dying back behind me. I had to race back, while my head burned with deadly knowledge of what I was into. It was a newspaper natural, newspaper dynamite. The killing of a gambler always is—and for us, it is real danger. We have to let honest gamblers operate—hell, we nurse them. Smothering gyps is all we can possibly hope to do. But try and explain that to the public—and try and keep reporters from hinting around. The headline BROADWAY GAMBLER SLAIN always has and always will sell papers. And it always has and always will stir to life every damned reformer and "league" in town to turn the heat on Broadway, as long as the story is in the public eye.

If Content would only name his killer, give us a chance to nail him fast and sweep the board clear so that there were no more news value—

I snapped my light alive again as I ran back into the garden. Content was lying with his face against the cement, his feet on the lower step of the little flight behind him. He was still breathing, but it was fainter now. I took the stairs at a leap, pushed the door wide open and flung down to his side again. Don't ask me where I got the strength to struggle with him, turn him over and get him up in my arms, stagger up and inside and lay him on the couch. I don't know myself.

I raked the place, spotted a cupboard and dived for it. It was the right one, full of bottles. I snatched the nearest—brandy— jerked out the cork as I ran back to his side.

It was wasted effort. His eyes had come open and were staring glassily at the skylight high in the roof. He had no pulse. He was dead.

I STOOD THERE a full minute, numbed, before I could rouse myself. I saw a phone in the corner and started for it with my head pounding. Halfway there I saw a fountain pen lying on the floor by the fireplace and a sheet of paper with a little writing on it a foot away. I reached for it—and I heard the back door of the apartment house come open across the garden, and then rasping steps coming across. I jumped for the door, half-closed it—and a Western Union messenger came running up the steps.

"Yes, sir," he said.

"What is it?"

"You phoned the office a few minutes ago for a boy to take a note to the Typhoon Club, didn't you?"

"To who at the Typhoon Club?"

He shrugged his shoulders. "I dunno. You just said to the—"

Somewhere I heard a siren start to wail and then stop abruptly. I stepped out and put my arm around his shoulders, turned him around away from the blood-streamers on the wall, stuck a bill in his hand, and led him down the steps. "It was a mistake, pal. We changed our mind. Hurry back and tell them nobody here called, will you?"

He went off looking blankly at the bill and I dived back inside. I used the phone first, called the little theater ticket agency off Times Square that functions as the Squad's unofficial headquarters. I got Al Hackett on the wire and ripped at him: "Dixie Higgins, the little tart the Marquis ran out. Put out a private wire for her—get her fast, it means a murder and a tough one. Get the word around fast but privately to locate her."

Then I pounced on the sheet of paper. The dead man had started the note without any salutation and gotten just two lines written before he was interrupted. The two lines were: *Well, it ended an hour ago and may that game haunt me the rest of my*

I stared at it. And I guess it was at that moment that my brain woke from its numbness and I had the first sharp wonder if Dixie Higgins *had* done this for sure. And the minute I questioned it, realization came with a jabbing rush that maybe she hadn't. Those pounding-on-piano noises—the shots! And she had been out of my sight only an instant through that back door when they went off! Was somebody else in here at that moment—somebody who had darted out and—I groaned and broke out in sweat as I ran to the door and looked at the not-too-high board fence at the side of the garden.

Game—haunt him—Typhoon Club. They tumbled in my hot brain. Tommy Content had been in some weird game—had been on the point of despatching a note about it to someone at the Typhoon Club—the latest of the expensive Tahitian South Sea night spots that had opened on Broadway. Could it be something connected with the game he was writing about that was behind his death?

I started for the door, and then swung back, furiously forcing myself down to sanity, getting hold of my wits. I stepped swiftly to the dead man's side, went through his pockets. I got absolutely nothing—and that was something in itself. He was a gambler, shrewd enough and smart enough to win the Marquis' O.K. Whether he had just been in a game or not, it was logical that he would carry a bankroll. If the weird game he had been in up till an hour ago had yielded him a big winning....

A fresh spasm of self-fury sweated me as I realized I had not reported the killing and I swung over to the phone again, hastily dialed headquarters and snapped: "Give me Homicide."

A SOFT, GENTLE voice behind me said, "Why, you've *got* Homicide, chum," and the door swung open on the skeleton-faced, green-eyed, meticulously dressed Lieutenant Lebaron—the one man on the whole force who would give twenty years of his life to dynamite the Broadway Squad.

I hung up slowly, and the gun in his fawn-gloved hand moved ever so slightly to draw my attention to it. Other faces appeared over his shoulder, and beyond and through his elbows I saw the glint of other guns.

"Just get the hands a little higher, Ace, there's a good boy. Is this him, Mr. Gallagher?"

The red-eyed face of the giant janitor pushed through. He was holding his jaw and his cheek was scraped and bruised.

"That's him, all right—come running in like a maniac with a gun—tried to kill me!"

I said: "Why you son of a—"

"Quiet!" Lebaron strolled over and looked down at the dead gambler. "Hmmm. Tommy Content. One of the thieves that work cozy with your little Squad, too. Tsk! Tsk! Too bad when old pals fall out, eh?"

I felt my face burn. Somebody outside said, "Here's the gun, chief," and Content's revolver was handed back in.

I said: "Listen, green eyes, don't get any ideas about trying to mix me in this."

"No?" He said in a surprised voice. "You mean you don't admit—"

"Can it!" I snarled. "You know damned well I had nothing to do with it. If that drunken fathead there has any wits, he'll tell you the shots went off in here, while I was wrestling with him back there in the hall."

Lebaron turned to look out the door. The now invisible janitor finally mumbled sourly: "I didn't hear no shots."

Lebaron looked quizzically at me with lifted eyebrows. There was evil joy in his green eyes.

I was purple. "O.K.," I said. "You're only half smart, Lebaron. The M.E. will be here in a minute and he'll make a nitrate test of my hand right here and now. Or if he hasn't the stuff, we'll go straight to the nearest precinct station. I'll put a stop to this crap fast. I—"

The parade broke on us, as the M.E.'s staff, the fingerprint men, the assorted experts trooped suddenly out of the apartment house back door.

"Get this," I snapped at Lebaron quickly. "I'm going to tell my story—and then I'm leaving. Either that or you're going to make a formal arrest."

The good humor whipped out of his face instantly, leaving it thin and grim and narrow-eyed. He didn't say anything. The flood of experts swept in.

He half-fumbled his cue by not letting me get my statement in for nearly twenty minutes. Half-fumbled it because by then I had my story straight in my own mind. I finally told the circle of them: "I was on my own beat and I saw this girl come hurrying down the street out front. She dropped what I thought was a pistol on the sidewalk. When I yelled at her, she snatched it up and ran in here, so I came after her—and that drunken Irishman snarled me up. When I came back here, Content was on the stoop out there dying and I carried him in here to try and bring him to. No, the girl vanished on me. She was short and plump and blond. I didn't see her face."

I stuck to it and they couldn't shake it. Lebaron backed down on the paraffin and, once I had declared my weight they made no effort to hold me. But—this was what Lebaron had been scheming for—the newspaper reporters could. Could and did. They were on the scene by now and they put me through the wringer, knowing I dared not offend them.

It was nearly an hour all told before I broke out finally and hurried down the block toward a drugstore to phone Hackett to meet me right away.

Even then, as I stepped out of the booth, the tall, hickory-straight inspector was standing there with his hands in his trench-coat pockets, his eyes heavy with worry. He took my arm and led me outside.

"For God's sake, Ace—what is this? Did you kill him?"

"No, no—but I've got someone who either did or who knows who did—was an eye-witness."

"You've *got* that person?"

"No," I groaned, "but I've got an alarm out. I'll break this, don't worry."

He let me go and shook his head worriedly. "You've got us all in a terrible spot if you don't—and quickly. Do you think it would be wise to wire the Marquis?"

"No, I don't. Just let me get at this," I blurted.

2

The Girl or the Game

HACK WAS WAITING for me three blocks down by a darkened automobile showroom. I shot at him as I came up: "Have you got the alarm out for—"

"Dixie. Yeah. I've done everything that can be done on that. What in God's name happened?"

I told him. He wiped sweat from his forehead. "My God," he said hoarsely. "We've got to—where are we going?"

"You're going in that drug store and phone the agency to try and locate the game that Tommy Content was in tonight."

"Eh? How?"

"Find out where games were held. I don't know. Comb the damned town. Shoot in there and tell every last damn guy on the Squad to get on the prowl and find out where *any* big games were tonight."

"What do you figure?" he asked huskily as he rejoined me and we went quickly down Broadway. "Tommy Content cleaned somebody and the guy was a bad loser?"

"It could be. Or he made a big win and somebody in the game tipped off a heister pal."

"Where are we going now?"

"To the Typhoon. Don't ask me for what. I don't know, but we have to check it."

It was just below Fiftieth. You go in, off Broadway, and up wide, shallow, carpeted stairs that turn you around and put you on a parquet with the checkrooms. The floor show was in full swing as we came up and we slowed to a halt at the draped entrance of the supper-room.

I don't know what it is about these places that has got them such popularity. Dim lights, a bar behind which water cascades steadily over green light, the pillars in the room disguised as tropical trees with electric-lighted fruit, a menu shaped and colored queerly, plus a special "house" drink that would ruin the stomach of an elephant—and there you are. Oh, yes, and a hula-hula flavor to the floor show. Just a flavor, that's all—one big number. That number was in full swing as we filtered up behind the headwaiter, Milo, and his captains.

I won't say it wasn't a nice number. Any number would be with Naomi Davies in it. That wasn't the name she worked under here, any more than it was the name she had headlined successfully under in the hey-dey era, before the South Sea tide swept in. Her coloring was made for *this* stuff—a sort of soft maplish skin she had, with huge soft doe eyes—brown—and electric black hair. She was a dancer, but her body was as soft and smooth and untouched-looking as beige velvet. She was small—I didn't realize how small until I saw her dancing there barefoot—gracefully curved. She was a tormenting little dish if you looked at her that way. She was also an expert, flawless dancer, no matter how you looked at her. Even in the grass skirt and going through the—to me—unlovely movements of the hula dance, she was dainty, flowing, graceful rhythm. Her voice was too soft and low to be very effective. They had three other hula maidens in the corners of the dance floor, strumming ukuleles and trying to give counterpoint to her undistinguished singing. They were nearing the end of the number.

They all slowly writhed backwards into what seemed to be a little stage set, boxed in—and as the song crescendoed to a finish, the little stage-set box slowly rose up and vanished into the ceiling, revealing the orchestra on a bandstand behind it.

The orchestra blared into a rhumba for dancing. I said, "Milo," and the headwaiter jumped, whirled, bowed twice and tried instantly to lead me away, over by the check-room.

"Nothing wrong, eh, Mr. McGuire?" he asked in an anxious undertone.

"No. I was just wondering if anyone had left word with you that they were expecting—"

I broke off as a man came down from the draped entrance to the supper-room, digging a handful of silver from his pocket and making for the row of phone booths against the wall. He was a stocky—even a chubby—little man of forty or so, with a round babyish forehead under his none-too-heavy blond hair. His eyes were cold, deep blue.

I SUPPOSE HE caught my eye because he was another gambler. Certainly not because he had a crooked bone in his body. He was Titanic Johnson, the tops as far as Broadway's corps of lone-wolf gamblers were concerned. He had been around as long as I had. He had never been accused of welshing, of breaking his word, or of crooked play. Don't mistake me. He was no saint. He couldn't be and last ten years on Broadway. Twice since I had been on the beat, I had heard rumors of someone either dead-beating him or attempting to cold-deck him. Nothing definite ever was heard or known but the parties involved just suddenly weren't around any more. None of this was recent. For the past five years, Titanic Johnson's name to a threat was enough to scare any grifter in the business clear to the other side of the globe, just as Titanic's name to an I.O.U. was as good as a treasury note.

I finished asking Milo my question when Titanic disappeared into a booth: "—expecting a message by Western Union boy?"

He looked pinched and anxious. "Why, I have a list of people expecting messages—phone messages, I had thought. But the propriety of showing the list to you, however—" he hesitated, fluttering his lips with his finger.

"O.K.," I said, and we went around behind the check-room where no one could see us and he gave me half a menu with penciled names scribbled in a column. They had the people's table numbers after them. They were a collection of celebrities and near-celebrities, none of which seemed to hold the slightest promise at this point.

"Did anybody happen to mention that they expected a message from Tommy Content? Or did anyone mention that name in any way whatever tonight?" I asked when I had glumly scrutinized the record.

"But no, Mr. McGuire, not tonight," Milo shook his head.

Walking back to the supper-room entrance, I jerked my head at the closed phone booth door. "Was Mr. Johnson here all during the floor show?"

"Oh, yes, Mr. Johnson had his dinner with us tonight. He has been here ever since."

I didn't have to ask, of course. Not whether he had been here during the show, that is. He was *always* here during the show—sitting in the darkest corner with his dark blue eyes glowing on Naomi Davies. Night after night, for nearly two years, I had seen him, in the various clubs where she had worked, always alone, his face as blank and expressionless as a mask, sitting watching her, only the glow of his eyes betraying his feelings. Not that anybody needed telling at this late date. It had become one of the famous Broadway romances.

Unfortunately, Naomi Davies had a husband—a cheap clarinet player in tenth-rate bands, out of work oftener than in, a vapid dumb little squirt with ears like a bat and a perpetually pursued expression on his thin, harried face. But for some incomprehensible reason she stuck to him. Titanic had tried everything—he wasn't very deft when it came to woman business—and was still nursing his wounds. He had offered to produce her own show for her, had proffered every expensive present he could think of—and got them smartly thrown in his face. He was unfortunately married himself—which was supposed to be why he had come to New York in the first place—and that was the one offer he was unable to make.

But everything else he had tried—even including one painful episode when he sent a couple of friends around to scare the meager Joe Davies out of town. The Marquis had had to intercede on that one, talk Titanic into tracking down the scooting clarinet player and bringing him back.

And yet, apart from these occasional interludes when she reached heights of fury I have never seen before or since in a woman, it was apparent that Naomi liked Titanic a good deal. But apparently that was all. Everybody—including me—was intensely curious to know how it would end. Certainly not by Titanic's withdrawal from the lists—that much was definite.

HE CAME OUT of the booth, walked over to the check-room and retrieved his hat, started out with his stolid little trudging walk. I said: "Oh, Titanic!"

He looked at me vaguely, then with recognition and stopped.

"You know Tommy Content, don't you?" I asked him.

"Yeah. Sure."

"You'd help me a lot if you know of any game he was in tonight—or maybe one that started last night and ran through?"

For all his expression gave me, I might as well have turned my back on him. "Hell, I don't know him well enough to keep tab on his games, Ace."

"I thought you might—well, maybe have been invited to play yourself, or like that."

"No. Sorry. Why?"

"He was killed tonight."

"Oh-oh." A worried line gradually came on his forehead as his cold, blue eyes searched mine. "I suppose that means the bluenoses—"

"Yeah. I want the lid on tight in the district—at least until the Marquis gets back."

He looked down at my shoe, rubbed his chin thoughtfully. "You know, that's a darned shame. He seemed like a pretty good youngster," was his verdict. "Who did it—or no, you wouldn't be asking me that question if you knew. Well, I hope you get him, whoever it is.

"My God," Al Hackett moaned as I watched Titanic disappear down the stairs. "Surely you're not going to suspect *him?*"

"Well, why not? One gambler goes down. Why not suspect another?"

"Yes, But *Titanic*—"

"I'm only kidding. I don't suspect anybody yet—except that

girl. Blind hell, how *can* I? Come on—let's get to work."

"Hey—the newspapers'll be on the streets inside an hour."

"What am I? A mental defective? I know goddam well they will."

THEY WERE GRUESOME. They could have been a little worse, but not much. War news had squeezed us out of the headlines but that was all you could say. We were there, in good solid position, in every sheet but one. With a unanimously keen sense of values, the boys had not even attempted to find synonyms for the three dependable words "Broadway," "gambler," and "slain."

One of them, a blazing critic of the city administration, had done a beautiful job on me. My name wasn't mentioned—I would have slapped a libel suit on them in twenty-four hours if it had been—but with "allegeds," "believeds" and "understoods" they had me halfway to the electric chair. And the hints of a general kind were starting—mention of "protected gambling," "rumored in Broadway circles," "known to be on surprisingly good terms with the Broadway police," and so on, far into the night.

This was not in the first editions—we had miraculously managed to escape that, but it was in the three o'clock issues, when I read through them under a street light across from our unofficial headquarters—the little theater ticket agency on Times Square.

I sweated. I was stopped cold till we could locate either the girl or this weird game mentioned in the dead man's note. I sweated all night, as a matter of fact, phoning, ranging up and down and across the section, driving the others to do the same.

It started to rain lightly and depressingly at four o'clock. I think I must have canvassed every hotel in the section in which professional games had *ever* been held. I uncovered one or two wild-goose chases—games that *had* been in progress the night before, but that, when I ran them down, had not contained Tommy Content. We couldn't get a break—unless you consider the painful conclusion to which we came, along about six, namely that the game, if any, had not been held in the Broadway district.

I wound up in the Marquis' apartment at eight o'clock, my head thick. I was soaked to the skin and I peeled off—I was camping out there while he was away—took a hot bath and went for a few hours sleep, feverishly half-convinced that we would *never* get an opening.

IT CAME ALMOST the minute I got back downtown. It was still raining when I ate in Lindy's at two, the sky dark and overcast. Most of the lights on Broadway were blazing in the gloom. I read the newspapers, squirming, while I ate, and we were still right up there.

When I walked into the narrow slot of the theater ticket agency, the three dicks that were in the back—Hackett, and the big blond giant, Johnny Berthold, and the frail-looking mummy-faced Kawelfoot—each looked up from a separate newspaper at me with uncomfortable eyes. They had got nowhere.

The call came on the Marquis' phone and a puzzled worried voice asked for him. When I said he was away but this was McGuire and could I help him, he said: "This is Lester Brandt, Mr. McGuire—at the Thorncliff Hotel branch of the Harvey Trust Company."

"Yeah." I vaguely remembered him as one of the Marquis "social"—I'll explain that in a minute—contacts.

"You know that chap that was killed last night—Tommy Content?"

I almost jumped into the mouthpiece. "Yeah? Yeah?"

"He carried an account with us, you know. And there is a chap here this afternoon trying to cash a four thousand dollar check drawn by Mr. Content. Whom should I notify?"

"Nobody, for the love of Allah! Just hold him—lock him in the vault—pile desks on him till I get there."

I called to Hackett and we hurried up and over—the Thorncliff is an actors' hotel located quite a piece west of Broadway in the Fifties—in a cab.

For years, I have kidded the Marquis about—and been secretly amazed and embarrassed at—the poor chump's attempts at social climbing. Not that he has ever gotten anywhere or ever will. But he has that one blind spot in his brain—in his heart of hearts he has some sort of a secret delusion that he is a gentleman. He schemes out shrewd campaigns to meet and be seen with fine people—socially prominent people—and struts like a peacock when he can manage it. Yeah, this is the Marquis I'm talking about, the little dapper, apparently sane, soft-spoken Marquis, with his quiet, expensive dark clothes—the toughest, shrewdest copper that Broadway ever saw—the Marquis, who was whelped in an Avenue A tenement. For five years, it had given us one private squirm after another, but what a dividend it paid us now—this Lester Brandt was the scion of a 1929-impoverished, but still veddy *Social Register* clan, on whom the Marquis had spread himself.

The bank was a shallow little affair in one corner of the

hotel—just big enough for a few tellers' windows above a marble case, and one executive's office. The branch was too small to rate a regular manager, but this Lester Brandt was the junior executive or whatever they call it, in charge. When the cab slopped us out into the streaming gutter and we hurried in, the mahogany office door by the entrance was closed tight and no sign of disturbance was visible. The special cop looked frowningly at us—I didn't know him—as we knocked at the door.

Brandt was a young blond man in a beautiful, long-pointed stiff collar. That is, he had other things on—a double-breasted blue suit, a tightly-knotted maroon knit tie, a gold class ring— but he was built around that immaculate collar. He had pale, corrugated hair and a good-looking blond face, on the sensitive side, which he poked anxiously out at us.

He moaned, as though he'd been holding his breath. "Oh, yes—Mr. McGuire! Come in, please!"

He stood aside to let us file in and hastily closed the door behind us. From a chair in one corner, a little shabby man with frightened bloodshot wary eyes jumped up and fairly squealed: "You can't do this to me! That check is O.K. I win it off him last night in a game!"

I looked at him, startled. He was a skimpy, undersized little runt. His ears stuck out like bat-wings. He was shaking, and sweating—maybe from fright and maybe from the liquor he had taken aboard a few hours previously. But there was no maybe about the fact that he was Joe Davies, the horn-tooting husband of Naomi Davies, the Typhoon Club dancer.

3

Gamblers Don't Talk

I DIDN'T EVEN try to put it together. A minute ago, the whole thing had been a closed book. Now it was split wide open—split into so many pieces that each one might be a pure gem in itself.

First I made sure. "The check is all right? There's nothing wrong with it?" I asked the blond Brandt.

"Of course it's all right," Joe Davies shrilled. "He even endorsed my sig in the—"

"Shut up. Is it all right, Mr. Brandt?"

The blond youngster dabbed at his forehead with a white handkerchief. "Yes, of course." His candid blue eyes looked anxious. "But of course we can't cash checks on—"

"I understand," I told him.

He swallowed, looked fearfully at the huddled little clarinet-player. "Is he—you don't suppose that this has anything to do with—"

"We're about to ask Mr. Davies all about it," I assured him grimly, "in the proper surroundings."

"No! No!" the excited little bloody-eyed Davies jumped back into the corner as I reached for him. "You can't do this to me! I'll sue you—I'll sue you for plenty! I win that dough—yeah, and plenty more—from Content last night! Look!" He hauled a wad of bills frantically out of his pants-pocket. It was laced with hundreds and fifties and there must have been an inch and a half of them. "I win twenty-nine grand from him, fair and square! You ain't going to touch me! I'll get a lawyer! I ain't going to no station-house!"

Hack's eyes met mine in groggy wonder. Then I said softly: "No, Joe—I guess we won't go to the stationhouse. Just somewhere where we can talk private!"

That sent him into a fresh spasm. He tried to fling himself deeper into his corner. "No, no—you want to roll me! I won't go—"

I slid the blackjack off my hip, balanced it delicately in my palm. "You won't be rolled. Mr. Brandt here has seen your dough and can vouch for what you had. Have him count it, if you like."

"I will! I will!" Hastily he flung the wad on the desk, begging the banker to go through it. Brandt hesitated, finally, at my nod, thumbed it through nervously.

"There's twenty-four thousand dollars there," he said in a startled voice.

"Twenty-*five*," screamed Davies. "Twenty-*five*—"

I snatched it up, jumped and got a hand in his collar, twisted it and crammed his wad into his side pocket. "Twenty-four, the man said, you little punk—now get out there before I slug you silly."

He cringed in sudden terror. "All right! All right! Don't—ah God, Ace, don't slug me—" He clasped his hands, almost went on his knees. I flung him toward the door and he stumbled.

"Stand up straight and walk like a man!" I snarled at him. "We're going out and into a cab and one false move and God help you!" I nodded to Hack and he opened the door with one hand, slid his arm through the shivering little musician's and we started out.

The bland young banker gulped desperately, and just at the very last minute, croaked, "Mr.—Mr. McGuire," and stepped back, nodding me again into the office. I waved Hack on and followed the banker. He was white-faced and sweating, running one finger inside his collar.

"Mr. McGuire—there's—there are a few funny things about that account. I—I don't know if they mean anything, but—I think it would be worth your while to get a court order for an examination."

"Yeah? Things like what, for instance?"

He winced, spread his palms. "Please—I can't possibly tell you unofficially. I—I'm beginning to wonder if I haven't put myself in a terrible position already. Please—please do it as I say. Of course, it may be nothing," he added hurriedly.

I looked at my watch. "Hell, it's nearly three. I couldn't get an order for a couple of hours anyway."

"I—I'll wait," he blurted. "The bank—we don't want to be mixed up—you understand?"

"Yeah. All right. There'll be somebody here from now on? O.K."

Hackett was in a cab with the shrinking Davies but I made a hand gesture to them and hurried into the hotel lobby, where I made a quick call to the agency. I got the big blond Johnny Berthold on the wire. He was the only one in and he isn't any too bright but he finally got what I wanted, promised to get the order from a judge we knew and bring it back and wait at the agency for me.

When I climbed in the cab, I gave the driver the address of the Marquis' apartment on Central Park West.

Davies cried frightenedly: "Where—where are you taking me?"

I leaned forward and slid the glass closed between us and the driver. "To somewhere where you'll be safe from what happened to the other winner in the game—Tommy Content."

"What? What happened to him?"

"He was shot to death last night in his little house."

HE SHOT STRAIGHT up in the air, clawing at his lips. Evidently Lester Brandt, with customary banker's discretion had not told him. He gibbered, stammered out frenziedly: "Oh God! Oh God! Where? When? Who—who shot him?"

"You shot him!" I snarled. "You think we're so dumb that we don't see that?"

He nearly went out of his mind. Tears were running down his cheeks as he clawed at my arm. "I didn't. I swear to God— listen to me! I swear—why would—"

I slapped him away. "Save that crap! Somehow—God knows how—you got into the game—"

"He invited me! He invited me to play—Tommy Content did."

"I'll believe that when wool grows in my hand. Somehow you connived into the game. Maybe you were ahead at one time—enough to cash that check for him. Then, in the end he went home with all the dough, including the check, and you saw a chance to knock him off and collar it."

"No, no!" He was going falsetto now. "No, I swear—I can prove—" I thought he was really going to blow his top.

Instead, he almost blew mine.

"I can prove I didn't steal it—I can—you've got to believe— and besides, he *didn't* quit winner. *Tommy Content didn't! He went home broke! He lost his wad!*"

I shook my head to clear it. "Waaa-itt a minute! Tommy Content went home broke?"

"Yes, yes! I—"

I snarled, "Shut up till we get inside," as we squealed in to the curb before the Marquis' apartment house. We rushed him upstairs and into the green-and-oak living-room. He was almost sobbing.

"Go on!" I prodded. "You say Tommy Content was cleaned. Who cleaned him?"

"*I* did! I swear I did!"

"All right," I said grimly, "you're riding a dream but put it this way—who *else* won besides you? Who was the big winner?"

"Nobody," he almost screamed. "I won—everybody else lost! That's what I'm telling you! I took them all!"

"Took who all? Who else were playing?"

He opened his mouth—and then suddenly he jerked his face into a tight little scowling knot. "I ain't saying. You oughta know better than ask me. Gamblers don't talk."

That was the prize. "Who ever told you you were a gambler?"

"That's all right. I'm a gambler and don't forget it."

"And you won't talk, eh?" I started for him.

"Wait!" Al Hackett said suddenly and looked at me with worried eyes. He started toward the bedroom, jerking his head. "Can I see you a minute, Ace?"

I growled: "You stay right where you are, gambler, if you know what's good for you."

Inside the bedroom door Hackett blurted: "Ace—that guy— you notice how he flushes and then gets pale, and all this talk— you don't suppose he's—"

"Well, what?"

"Well, off his head or something. He doesn't act natural."

"It's the dough, stupid. He never saw fifty bucks before in his life. He's dough-happy."

I walked back with my lips tight, walked to where he was standing in the middle of the rug, smacked him a good poke in the side of the jaw that slammed him halfway across the room and piled him down in a corner.

"All right, gambler," I said. "Who was in that game besides you and Content?"

He was sobbing and hiccuping at the same time. He choked out wailingly: "Charlie Pfluger and the two Ottheimer brothers."

"Where was the game?"

"At—at Pfluger's place on—on Long Island."

LONG ISLAND! NO wonder we couldn't get a line on it. I growled, "That's more like it," and started for the door. Then I stopped and came back and stood over him.

"Now get this, stupid! For all I know Tommy Content may have been killed in mistake for you. Maybe somebody's out gunning for you right now."

He grabbed at my trouser. "Oh God, Ace—no! No! Why would they?" He clawed himself up to his knees. "No—no— you're trying to scare me!"

"I'm telling you the truth. You're safe as long as you're here, but the minute you go out on the street—What time are you due to toot that horn of yours tonight?"

"I ain't going! I quit the job this morning."

"O.K., then—you can stay here till we get back. Don't open the door to anybody. Anybody that's entitled to get in will have a key, understand? You can get yourself something to eat and drink in the kitchen, but don't get stewed. I may need you sober. Get it?" I said.

"Yes, yes," he sobbed again. "Oh, God, Ace—they—they got no call to kill me—"

"What call did they have to kill Tommy Content?"

"Oh, I dunno, I dunno!" he wailed.

"Well, there you are," I said and we went out, leaving him there. Hack started for the elevator, but I blurted, "Wait a minute. I got to think," and backed over into a wooden love seat and sat down. I put my palms to my head.

I *had* to think. The crazy twists to this thing were piling up too fast. It was historic—if even a part of what the cloud-riding little punk in the apartment had said were true. Nobody on Broadway would believe it—believe that Joe Davies, the literal definition of the word "dope," had sat into a game with Tommy Content, Charlie Pfluger, and the Ottheimer brothers in the first place. Or clipped them in the second place. Charlie Pfluger was the king of the hat-check concessionaires—with a heart as cold as a .45 barrel against your neck. The Ottheimer brothers *ran* Detroit gambling. And Tommy Content knew all the answers in the back of the book. Lady Luck must have had convulsions in handing the win to the little horn-tooter. No wonder Tommy Content had said that game would haunt him....

I couldn't quite believe it was true. But if it were—what? Could my carelessly tossed-off line to Davies back inside— that Tommy Content had been killed in error for Joe Davies— have a grain of truth in it? Might the heister who had been waiting to waylay the winner of the game have gotten his lines crossed somewhere?

Or—torturing thought—was I entirely off the track? In spite of all my efforts to dig up a game that Tommy Content *had* been in, was his death entirely unconnected with it after all?

I wouldn't face that—yet. There were still too many queer little angles. And maybe I was falling for a hunch, if the truth must be known. There was no reason why the whole sequence that bothered me couldn't be pure coincidence—starting with the note in Tommy Content's studio, our going to the Typhoon and seeing Naomi Davies and Titanic Johnson there, then the circle bending around again by the discovery of Joe Davies attempting to cash one of the dead Tommy's checks—Joe, the husband of the delectable Naomi, who was herself the object of the town's biggest gambler's torch-carrying—

No, there was no reason why it had to spell anything—but I couldn't shake off the conviction that it did. *If* what Joe Davies had claimed were true.

I got up and told Hackett: "Come on—we've got to make dead sure he didn't just dream all this."

HE HADN'T. WE located Charlie Pfluger in his apartment on Central Park South. He was a benign-looking little monkey-faced man with a high color, little tufts of feathery white hair on the top and sides of his gleaming red scalp and mild, kind blue eyes. He received us, beaming, in his expensively furnished cream and maroon sitting-room, rubbing his hands.

"Well, boys, well, well," he said hospitably.

"About the poker game you were in up till last evening," I said.

He beamed even more. "Sorry, Ace, you must have the wrong party for once. Don't play poker—or any other games of chance. Haven't for years."

"Tommy Content made a dying statement and Joe Davies just cracked."

"Oh." He said it a little dispiritedly. "Well?"

"We hear—and can't believe—that Joe Davies quit the big winner with everybody else losing."

He rubbed the tuft over his right ear vigorously with his fingers, looked a little troubled. "Well, it's the truth, though even *I* find it hard to believe. Yes, it's the truth."

"How much did you go for?"

"Very little—about eleven hundred. The Ottheimer boys probably dropped eight or nine thousand—and Tommy Content the rest. It wasn't a very big game," he added apologetically.

"You don't think Tommy was killed because of anything that happened at the game?"

"Eh? No! Good Lord, no! It was all very innocuous, as you can plainly see from the amounts that changed hands." But he still looked a little bleak.

We located the Ottheimers in the Park Vista Hotel on Seventh Avenue—well inside our district.

They were a queer pair—and pair is the word. Moe was big, swarthy, with coal-black, muddy eyes and oiled black hair. His bony, wide-shouldered frame looked as though it had been developed carrying ice. Mert was a little thinner, a little shorter, but his dark face had been cast in the same mold, the mold in the meantime having become just a little warped. But his eyes had that same muddy, deceptively stupid look, his lips the same full redness as his brother. They came to the door of their room, both wearing identical blue trousers and white collar-attached silk shirts. And each had a knotted black silk four-in-hand tie that was pulled down the identical distance on the shirt front, from the unbuttoned collar. They both knew me, all right, but they gave no sign of it, just stood staring blankly at us through the crack of the door.

"Open up," I told them. "Want to ask you some questions about last night's game."

They did not move, just gave us the same muddy stare.

I snarled: "Unless you'd rather answer them down at the precinct-house."

After a second, they used mental telepathy or something and stepped back grudgingly. Moe, in the rear, dropped something tinkling to the floor, made a quick grab for it and had to pursue it halfway across the room before he could get his spatulate brown fingers on it. It was a round piece of glass. He returned to his exact relative position behind his smaller brother.

"How much did you lose in the game that wound up last night?" I asked when we were inside.

Mert looked up inquiringly over his shoulder at his brother's face, then back dully at us. "What game?"

"Skip that! Tommy Content talked before he died. Joe Davies gave us an earful and I've just come from Charlie Pfluger."

"Oh." It was exactly the same sound as Pfluger had made.

"We understand Tommy Content was the big winner," I hazarded.

They shook their heads together.

"Who was, then?"

"Davies. Davies."

I looked incredulous. "You mean that little dope took you guys?"

"Yeah."

"For how much?"

"I lost seven, Moe six," Mert said. "Tommy Content dropped around twenty. Charlie Pfluger broke even. Any more questions?"

I tried to think of one. "No, I guess not," I said. "Don't leave town."

Moe opened his mouth quickly, then closed it and returned to staring at us blankly.

All this had used up time. It was after four. We went down to the lobby of the hotel, called the agency to see if big Johnny had gotten back with the court order yet. He hadn't and we walked on slowly down to wait for him. The rain was coming down in steady driving force now, the sky as black as twilight. We hung around the agency for nearly half an hour before Johnny came in. I took the order from his hand and told Hackett: "I don't know what this is. I think I'm going nuts. But you stick here in case anything comes on that damned girl. Then I rode again up to the bank, alone.

The shades were drawn on the shallow little branch bank this time, but a bowl fixture in the ceiling inside was alight and, to my rattling, the pale blond head of the collared Lester Brandt came bobbing out of the office.

He was tired and worried looking when he let me in, and said fretfully: "I almost thought you weren't coming." He locked the door again behind us and led me into the office.

"You got—" he began anxiously as he sat in his chair, and broke off as I tossed the court order across to him. Some relief showed in his sensitive blond face and his reddened eyes looked grateful. He tendered me a pack of checks, bound around with a blue bank statement. "I had the bookkeeper make up the statement as of the close of business today," he told me.

I said we reaped a dividend from knowing this youngster. It was the relative size of a pea to a bushel basket compared to the astounding news I got now.

4

Irish Luck

THE FIRST SHOCK was when I unfolded the blue statement and glanced curiously at the final figure. It was thirty-four thousand dollars odd. That wasn't too amazing—except that it was in red and the legend in the column opposite it read: *Overdraft*.

I said: "Good God Almighty, do you allow gamblers to carry overdrafts of—"

"Look at the top of the sheet," he told me.

I looked. Printed in book-keeping machine letters across the extreme upper edge of the form was: *Account guaranteed by T.T. Johnson.*

Guaranteed by Titanic Johnson! The murdered man's account had been backed by Titanic Johnson! It was astounding. Titanic Johnson, who had rather absently told me in the Typhoon last night that he knew the dead man slightly! It turned the whole crazy business around.

The banker was mopping at his neck with a handkerchief, eyeing me miserably. "I—I hope you'll never report that *I* drew your attention to all this. I don't know how the bank would feel, but they wouldn't like it. I—will you go through those checks and—of course, I don't know the man's affairs but"—he almost choked before he blurted it out—"if you'll notice—nearly every check in that whole pile is made out to a woman—every big check, that is."

"A woman! Gentle hell! Who?"

"A—a Miss D'Estelle."

I almost spilled the checks as I hastily snapped the elastic band off them, hastily shuffled them.

They were there—God knows they were there. Five thousand. Ten thousand. Eight thousand. Twelve thousand. Four thousand. The smallest was twenty-five hundred and they amounted to over sixty G's all told.

I said: "Do you know this woman—this Mary D'Estelle?"

"Yes. Yes. Mr. Content brought her in and introduced her to me when he—when she cashed the first check. If you'll notice, they all bear only *her* endorsement—weren't deposited anywhere. She just came in and cashed them.

"How long has this been going on?"

"Just—just this last month, as far as I know."

"If he has been handing her so much why isn't the overdraft larger? Oh, I see. He has been making deposits, too."

"Both Mr. Content and Miss D'Estelle have made deposits," he assured me anxiously.

"The girl too? She's been depositing—"

"Yes."

I was completely out of words. Titanic Johnson standing behind Tommy Content's account, guaranteeing it. Tommy handing money in large chunks to a woman—and the woman occasionally putting it back.

"What's this woman like?" I snapped. "Young?"

"Yes. Quite young—and most attractive. I would say that she was Spanish, except that she has eyes of a queer shade of blue. She has black hair and combs it that Spanish way—you know—parted in the middle and drawn tight, sort of. She—

she has a beautiful figure and a really regal carriage. Each time I have seen her she had on a jacket of that black-and-white monkey fur and—"

I nearly choked. I jumped to my feet. "You don't know where she lives, or—"

"Yes. Yes, I believe I do. If I may—" He reached over and took the checks, riffled them quickly and drew one out. He turned it back up and put it before me. "The first time she came in alone to cash one, I scribbled it down there."

Beside the pinched, crabbed vertical *Mary D' Estelle*—the signature was composed entirely of little straight lines, it seemed—he had penciled: *Apt. 3B, 156 W. 23rd Street.*

I was on fire—but then a sudden fresh idea checked me. "Wait! Have you any idea whether Titanic—that's Mr. T.T. Johnson—knows about all this?"

"I have no idea, no."

"Do you keep him posted on what goes on in this account?"

"No. He did not request us to, except at the end of the month. He will, of course, receive a duplicate statement—end-of-month statement—day after tomorrow."

He hesitated, and then burst out: "Mr. McGuire—I hope you appreciate that I am undoubtedly exceeding my authority in telling you all this. I'm most uncomfortable about the whole thing, but—well, I *want* to get things cleared up and—"

"Do you want it enough to come down and help pick this woman out for me?"

He fairly cringed. "Oh. Good Lord, I—" His Adam's apple bobbed and his strained eyes met mine. He had a refusal on his lips.

"You don't have to show yourself," I forestalled him quickly.

"Just be somewhere so you can tell me if I've got the right party—if I do get her."

"What—what are you going to do to her?"

"It depends on what answers she can think up."

He mopped distractedly at the inside of his collar and then finally agreed to go. "You—you're going when?"

"Right now."

He winced again, stood up and mopped his hands, agonized for seconds, and finally croaked, "Well, all right," and reluctantly got his hat and fly-fronted covert coat from a cupboard.

"I—I have my car here," he said miserably as we left the office. "Suppose I drive you down and then just—just sit in the car and—"

"Fair enough."

We ran out through the now pelting, lashing rain and into his year-old Buick coupé at the curb. He kicked the starter and we pulled away, trundling westward. "I'll go down on the ramp," he said, and then got jittery again. "Mr. McGuire—you understand that if the bank knew I was going so far out of my way to—"

"Forget the bank. They'll know nothing from me."

We were almost alone on the half-awash street. The rain had chased most of the traffic to cover.

I TRIED TO run the thing through my hot brain as we bounded along on the elevated roadway. It was like a vast merry-go-round—a dozen things to watch at the same time, coming slowly round and round. Tommy Content shot to death. Tommy Content with the phone number of the Typhoon. Titanic—this item had expanded a little now—Titanic *in* the

Typhoon. But also I had to consider that Naomi Davies was there, too. Joe Davies, winning from Tommy Content—Joe Davies, who was all that stood between Titanic and Naomi Davies. I almost found myself wondering if Titanic, having tried everything else, could have deliberately set out to murder the worthless little musician and had, by some error, cut down Tommy Content instead.

That was too feeble. But in thinking of it, another possibility much more sane popped up. Titanic had guaranteed Tommy Content's financial operations. Presumably it was a business arrangement. He was staking the younger man, in other words, till he got started in the big town. But Tommy Content had picked up Dixie Higgins—I was positive she was this Mary D'Estelle—had been playing catch with huge chunks of cash—really Titanic's cash when you got down to it—with the girl. What if Titanic had somehow found out about that? What if, in some way not yet quite clear, the larcenous girl and Content were working a racket on Titanic and the deadly, dead-pan little master-gambler had wised up?

I realized that I was trying to force it—that I was not in close enough yet to try and make the hook-up. I don't apologize for it.

Forcing has always been my theory. When we get a murder like this—there it lies. The person who killed Tommy Content must have known that we would be jerked into the picture—that we would have to make extra effort to break the job. That person would be waiting, watching. I won't say that I believe every murder has a flaw in it. Maybe. But this *is* positive—no killer can ever be sure that *his* murder hasn't a flaw in it.

A hundred times I have seen it work—seen the killer, driven more and more nervous by pounding, driving effort on our part, get the fidgets. If we can get one or two breaks and drive in, there is a chance to force him to action. Some action, any action—it doesn't matter, just so it provides a fresh trail, one that is unconsidered. And—with the checks in my possession, with the really solid things I had uncovered—it seemed incredible that I couldn't force some action here.

It came so fast that it was as though Fate had just been holding a bludgeon over me till I had reached that point in my thinking.

We were approaching the Twenty-third Street exit—the narrow, precipitously-sloping little slot that dumps you down into the cluster of steel ramp pillars on West Street below. I said to Brandt: "Did this woman—" and that was as far as I got.

God knows how either of us lived!

He angled the car over to the exit lane—and it bucked once. He trod on the brake—and we almost went into a skid. He choked: "What the—" as we half slid, tipping onto the incline. He gasped, wrenched the wheel. I saw his eyes go big as he cried out wildly, *"Wheel—doesn't turn—steering gone,"* and we raked the side of the slot, bounced. He made a queer whimpering sound. We thundered downward, slammed from side to side. His hands seemed to go fluttery-crazy of their own accord as terror drained his face. *"God—steering gear—gone— jump. For God's—"* he screeched as we hurtled to the bottom. In crazy panic he grabbed the emergency brake with one hand, snatched at the door-handle with the other as steel pillars leaped into the headlight beam. I tried to grab my door—the car went into a wild, whirling skid—and the world dissolved in a thunderous, brain-splitting explosion. I was flung far out into a fire-splitting, roaring blackness.

AGES LATER, IT seemed, I began to spin back. Just before I opened my eyes, I heard someone miles away exclaim: "By God—this steering knuckle has fresh wrench marks! This car's been tampered with!"

A million slickered cops seemed to be moving about in light beams when I looked. The red eye of an ambulance glowed. People were shouting. A white-coated interne was bending down over me—I was on a stretcher and he was trying to feel my spine under me.

I croaked, "I'm all right. Let me up—" and his hand jumped to my chest.

"Lie still," he snarled at me. "Why you're alive God knows. You must have *something* broken," he added in a complaining voice.

"What about my friend?" I croaked at him. "Leggo of me. I'm all right." I fought my way to a sitting posture. Half my face was numb and to breathe was like lifting a thousand-pound weight on my right side. One hand was covered with bandages and there was a strip across my cheek.

"Your friend's got a broken arm and some broken or cracked ribs and a nice gash in his face. He may have a fractured skull—we don't know."

I got my eyes in focus—and I suddenly looked down at my hand. Then my hand flew frantically to my inside pocket. I tried to spring up in panic—and reeled squarely into the interne's arms. But the weakness was only a minute, and then I was looking around me desperately.

I did not have to look far. They were in an immense pool of water, not five feet from me, floating loosely, scattered, being whipped by rain that was slanting in under the ramp structure—the checks.

I dived for them, moaning to myself, went to my knees in the water, clawing them to me.

I could have saved the trouble. They were drenched, their faces no more than vague blurs on which even the printed name of the bank was no longer visible. As evidence, they were done for.

I SHOULD HAVE been sunk. I wasn't. The evidence was gone—but I had driven the killer to action. I had him moving again—afraid of me, whoever he was. If I could press in, blast out—

Al Hackett's voice said hoarsely, "Ace! Ace! Are you all right?" as he and big Johnny burst through the crowd. "Ace—you madman—get into that ambulance!"

I let them help me to my feet, then I slapped their arms away and said grimly: "Ambulances, hell. Let me out—"

I saw Lester Brandt, being lifted in a stretcher and my conscience gave me a stab. His arm was in splints and there was a bandage around his head. I got over and stopped the stretcher carriers. His eyes looked up at me in fright.

I said awkwardly: "I'm sorry I sucked you into this."

"That's all right," he croaked feebly. "But—were they trying to kill me for helping you or—"

"No, no," I assured him hastily. "Nothing like that. Just after me, that was all."

Did I believe it? I certainly did not. The minute I thought of it, I began to get the jitters about the poor devil's safety. I spun away as the stretcher moved on. "Johnny!" He hurried over and I snapped at him: "Ride that stretcher! Guard that guy—and I mean guard him!"

"Huh? You mean this—you mean somebody's trying to get him?"

"It may be so. For God's sake, don't let him get killed on us—or we'll all be walking beats again. Grab anybody suspicious that comes near him."

"Sure. O.K." He trotted off.

"Get me to a drink, fast," I muttered to Hackett, and he had sense enough not to argue, merely set about beating a way out of the crowd for me—in a direction opposite to where the ambulance lurked. I was pretty giddy, but by the time I had downed a triple Scotch in a bar a little piece across Twenty-third I was feeling the blood surge back into me.

"What in God's name happened?" Hackett blurted.

"Somebody's fixed the steering knuckle on Brandt's car. I guess because they saw him getting chummy with me."

"Who did it? Have you any idea?"

"No, but I'm getting awfully close to finding out," I said as I stood up from the bar. "The same person that killed Tommy Content, needless to say—and I think I've got him on the run. This thing is going to be all over quick—or I miss my guess.

"You better beat it up to the Marquis' place and keep an eye on that little punk Davies. The killer is moving now and I'm still blank on the whys and wherefores. For all I know, killing Davies might work in here somewhere. And you might put one of the boys on nosing around in front of the Thorncliff Hotel. Brandt's car must have been standing there all day—practically right in front of the bank—and somebody might have noticed something or seen it being tampered with."

"Where are you going?"

I said from memory—burning memory—"Number one-five-six West Twenty-third Street—apartment 3B—where we were headed before this thing happened. There's a dame named D'Estelle in on this—and she may be the key-log in the jam. Never mind any more questions—go on up and get beside that punk while I kick this thing over."

I watched him whirl away in one cab and then I grabbed another. There were still lights, crowds, commotion, a block and a half over under the ramp. I went away from there—it was far enough to where I was going so that I wouldn't have walked it even if I weren't sopping wet and bruised from head to foot. As I shot crosstown, I reflected, not for the first time, on the toughness of the McGuires, and the luck of the Irish that kept me still alive.

5

Emergency Ward

IT WAS AN apartment house, along the style of Greenwich Village. That is, it had no lobby, but only a narrow carpeted cramped hall inside the vestibule door. There were bells and I reached for them but before I rang any I found the door was not locked and I pushed in.

The light had burned out in the lower hall and I had to pick my way from what illumination came down the stairs. I figured 3B would be on the third floor, and it was.

There were two apartments to a floor. The building was an ancient converted house, far from being a lower-class outfit, although not a rich man's dwelling. The carpets were thick and good, the walls plastered in immaculate cream, with standing lamps in little wall niches. The door of 3B had two locks on it—one a turnbolt affair, the other the old-fashioned mortise.

I knocked and got no answer. I did that three times. Then I picked the lock and went into a room smelling of stale cigarette smoke. I found a light switch beside the door and clicked it on.

I was in a living-room with a fireplace, a Chinese rug, brass around the mantel, a daybed covered with a black silk spread with a red dragon on it, four comfortable arm and wing chairs and end-tables against everything. It was a room from which somebody had departed for good.

Don't ask me how I knew that. Just a feeling, or possibly a conclusion from the total absence of anything portable that a person would live with. There was another room—a bedroom. With a desperate sinking feeling, I saw that the bed was unmade, a telephone on a bedside table. The bureau drawers were partly open—and bare.

In consternation, I prowled hastily round the two rooms looking for *anything*.

I don't know why I didn't think about the telephone at once, but it was minutes before it occurred to me and I jumped quickly in and lifted the receiver.

It hummed—the dial tone. That surprised me. I quickly dialed an official and told him who I was. "Who, what, when and where?" I asked him, and got nothing more than I already knew, for my pains. The phone was listed for Mary D'Estelle, had been installed three months ago and no notice had been received to date to disconnect it.

It was when I hung up, a little desperately, and went to put the handset back that I noticed the little penciled figures shining against the black base of the instrument. I snatched it up again—and could read a Bryant number plainly. I hesitated just a minute before I dialed the number.

A voice that I recognized as clearly as I would have my own answered quickly. I said, "Hello? Who is this?" in a growl.

"This is Tommy Content," Lieutenant Lebaron told me, "Who—"

I slammed it down viciously. Leaving the door of the apartment open I went out and downstairs. Looking at the bells and letter boxes in the vestibule got me the information that the superintendent lived in 1A. I groped my way to the back of the dim-lit first floor and knocked.

A door opened and I could make out a short, fat woman in

a hallway that was also unlighted. Vague glow filtered around a corner from a room beyond.

I said: "This Miss D'Estelle that lived in 3B. Do you know where she's gone?"

She put hands on hips and said furiously, "For the love o' the church, are you deaf? I told you I didn't even know she'd moved out until you told me, but it appears that Danny O'Reilly run a trunk up for her in his truck—"

"Wait a minute!" Chills ran up my back. "Wait a minute! Who did you tell this to? When?"

"To yourself, who else—not half an hour ago."

"You didn't tell me—" Getting accustomed to the dim light, I looked down and saw she had a picture in one hand, framed in leather. There was a woman in the picture with hair parted in the middle and drawn tight back. "Wait a second—*that* isn't her, is it?"

"Sure and it is. After you told me she was gone I went up and found she'd left."

"May I see it?" I flashed a badge on her and she almost fell over backwards.

"Good Lord, and is she—come in—come in."

I WENT IN and looked at the picture. That finished the last doubt that Mary D'Estelle was Dixie Higgins!

I demanded: "Who did you say took her trunk? Where can I—"

She got very excited. "Danny O'Reilly—three doors down! He has a truck and she got him to take—ring Mrs. O'Reilly's bell."

I swung back out to the street and down to a square, yellow-stucco structure whose just-below-ground-level floor housed a bric-a-brac shop piled with counters. There was a little arched entrance to the apartments above and I found a fly-specked, handwritten *O'Reilly* card slanting drunkenly in one of the bell slots. There was no advertising of the trucking business. I jabbed the bell.

The door remained silent. I rang—and rang again—and again. And then finally, when I was sweating blood, it clicked and I piled in.

A raucous woman's voice called down the stairs: "Yeah? Who is it?"

"I want Danny O'Reilly," I called back as I went up to where a terrific old Irishwoman stood wiping her hands on an apron.

"Do you? And who are you?" and when I flashed the badge hastily, "Saints preserve us! They've already taken him to the hospital!"

"*What!* What happened? What hospital?"

"Why, the feller rang for him and called him down and they went out in the back yard to talk and then his poor mother heard him moaning and groaning out there a while later and she went out and he was beat to ribbons."

"Did anybody see the man that did it?"

"No, not a soul. He just called up. He had a nice quiet voice and—"

"What hospital did they take Danny to? Quickly—this is urgent."

A slow look of stupidity spread over her face. "Why, now," she said blankly, "That's funny. I—I didn't ask. She just put him in a taxicab and—maybe it was Mercy—or no, I think it was—mister, I don't know where and that's a fact."

I damned near went nuts. I raced out and found the nearest drug store and started calling hospitals like mad. I had to refuel from the cash register eight times, before I had run through the list—and Danny O'Reilly wasn't registered in any. I knew what that meant—that he was in some emergency ward and that his card hadn't reached the file yet—and the knowledge drove me batty. I had to stall—and then start calling them all over again. A whole hour dropped away while I feverishly dialed, rattled questions—and then I found him.

I found him in—you guessed it—St. Thomas's, the same establishment to which they had taken Lester Brandt and had done their best to take me.

I burst in there in ten minutes flat, shot at the nurse in charge: "Danny O'Reilly—accident patient—life and death—police!"

A second nurse, bent over a file a few feet away turned on me and said wonderingly: "Why—they just put him in my ward. Come—I'll take you."

I grabbed her arm and we trotted to the elevator, rode up four floors and then strode on along a corridor. "What happened to him?" I asked.

"Why, it looks as if someone had deliberately beaten him in the face with a steel rod or something like that. He has a bad concussion, but we don't think a fracture. The X-rays don't—"

"Is he conscious?"

"No, he's delirious."

WE HURRIED INTO the ward. There was a screen around one bed and we got around it. Two white-coated internes were looking down at the moaning, babbling youth who was twitching his heavily-bandaged head around on the bed.

One of the docs looked at me as though I weren't there and told the other: "I'll give him a shot of morphine."

I said, "You will like hell. You'll give him a shot of adrenalin."

They looked at me scowling. "Who the hell—"

I flashed my badge. They made contemptuous shooing motions with their hands together. "Beat it, oppercay."

"Listen," I hastily appeased. "That guy's got to talk—even if just a minute. I got to know who did it to him."

The shooing motions went on. "We can't hear a word you say," one of them drawled.

"Look," I pleaded. "It isn't just him. He was beaten to get a certain address out of him. The man who got it wanted the address to go kill a girl. I swear that's the truth. If I can get it in time myself, I can stop a murder. That's God's truth."

It won. Their scowls melted to looks of concern. They hastily consulted each other's eyes and one said: "Well, it oughtn't to do him any good but it won't kill him." And they sent a nurse scurrying.

"Back out a few minutes," they told me. "We'll call you when he can speak—five minutes, say. You can't blow questions at him till we set him."

I backed out—and found I was still holding the picture of Dixie Higgins in my hand. I put my face in and said: "I'm going up to see a patient in the private rooms a minute. I'll be right back. I ran out to the nurse's desk in the hall. She told me where Brandt's room was and I was whisked up to it and knocking on the door in seconds.

Big Johnny came out belligerently, a hand in his pocket.

"Oh-Oh—it's you, huh? What?"

I pushed on past him. Lester Brandt was sitting on the edge

of the bed in trousers and shoes. I said: "Well, you don't look so bad."

His smile was none too strong. "Oh, no. I'm all right—except for the arm."

I showed him the picture. "Is this your Mary D'Estelle?"

And then my heart ran down into my boots as he looked at it and said, "No," and then, "Wait a minute," dubiously, frowningly. He stared at it for minutes. "Well, yes, it looks like her, at that," he said slowly. "But—well, yes I guess—"

"My God," I moaned, "You've got to be sure. It means everything!"

He wanted to be, but he couldn't be. I fairly danced in torment, while he argued himself back and forth.

Finally, I burst out: "Listen—I expect to know any minute where *this* girl is. If she's your Mary D'Estelle, I've got to know it. How sick are you?"

"I—I'm all right, really. This arm—and I look bad, but I—"

"Can you get dressed and come with me? I'll promise you I won't expose you to any danger or anything, but I've got to have you there."

"I—yes, yes, I could—" and then the shadow of apprehension came into his eyes. "You don't think that they'll—"

"They won't harm you. I'll take care of you," I promised.

"But they won't let me out of here. And my clothes—all but these are destroyed."

I set my jaw. "Johnny'll smuggle you out. Where do you live?" and when it turned out to be Gramercy Park, "Johnny can take you over there—right now—for clothes, and then you meet me in front of here as soon as you can. I have to wait here for five minutes."

"All right," he said, without enthusiasm.

We got him down the fire stairs and I hurried back down to the ward and nearly went crazy.

It was nearer fifteen minutes when the sobbing voice of the young Irishman finally told me: "I took her trunk up to 3282a Riverside Drive for her. She gave me ten bucks not to tell. The other fellow beat it out of me."

"What other fellow?" I raved. "Did you see him? What did he look like?"

"I dunno—big—I just saw his eyes and he started to slug me with his gun."

The doctors grabbed me, flung me out.

I groaned, ran out and buzzed the elevator. When I ran out into the rain, the cab was waiting where I had arranged for them to meet me. I jerked open the door and flung at Johnny: "Go on back up there and maybe fool them into thinking he's still there, till we get back." And when he had stumbled out and I had dived in to take his place, I gave the cabby the Riverside Drive number.

WE RACED THROUGH the streaming night. The banker beside me was shrunken and shriveled. He spoke only once, bitterly, on the crazy ride up. "I wonder whether I'll still have a job at the bank when this is all over. They're likely to— all this publicity—"

"Hell, you'll be a hero—bring in business," I assured him. "Don't worry."

We flung to a stop in front of a mammoth, ten-year-old apartment house and I jumped out. "You can sit here if you like," I told him, but he was eeling out after me hastily.

"No, no," he said anxiously. "I—I'll feel much safer if you'll let me trail along with you."

I waited only a minute before I said: "All right."

I didn't fool in this building. I got the superintendent out of his basement, flashed my badge and read the riot act to him. "Keep your mouth shut and hand me your pass-key, or I'll have you blackjacked to death," I told him.

We rode to the eleventh floor—she had moved into a furnished place there five hours ago and was still in, I was tremblingly assured, under the name of Carla Montanez.

And then we were in the hall, treading noiselessly on carpet.

Her apartment was at the very end of the hall.

6

Take it Away

I DIDN'T KNOW just what to do. I hesitated. I bent down to try and peek through the keyhole, but all I could see was light—and what seemed to be the edge of a Murphy bed.

Then, to prop myself while I turtled my neck around, I put a hand on the floor—and it was wet.

Somebody had entered here, not an hour ago—not long enough ago to have the water he—or she—had shed—dry out yet.

That decided what I would do.

I put my mouth to Brandt's ear and whispered: "Go down one of the halls and wait there. I'm going in and I don't know just who's there." But he shook his head in hasty negative, jabbed a finger at the floor to indicate that he would stay just where he was.

I shrugged. Then I set about inserting the key noiselessly in the lock. I guess it took me two full minutes. Then I stood up, took the gun from my hip and spent a minute more turning the key—and then found the door was unlocked. I raged inwardly, got the knob, got it turned round—and went in.

There were two people in the one-room apartment. I snapped: "Freeze—don't move!"

Nobody moved. Titanic Johnson, standing by the daybed had a nail brush in one hand and was holding the long, tapered fingers of a girl in the other. The girl lay on the daybed, her dark hair parted in the middle, drawn back tightly behind her head, her skin like wax. She stared unseeingly up at the ceiling.

She would never see again. Dixie Higgins was stone dead, her white throat a mass of bruises and scratches. Her dress was torn a little in the front.

Titanic opened his mouth and I snapped: "Shut up! Get your hands high and turn around."

He looked at me with a wooden face, slowly obeyed, still holding the nail brush. I made a quick grab for his hip, got the short black automatic from where I knew he always carried it. It still had dried blood on the muzzle.

I backed over to shut the door—and almost backed into the goggling Brandt.

I pulled him inside impatiently. "All right. You're safe now. Titanic's not a cop-killer, are you, Titanic?"

He didn't answer. I didn't expect him to. I went over and picked up the dead girl's hand. Her fingernails were shiningly spotless, paintless.

"You can put your hands down," I told Titanic, and backed a little away from him.

Titanic turned and faced me. I thought his eyes started a little when he saw Brandt over my shoulder.

"So," I said. "You're the guy that doesn't know Tommy Content well enough to keep tab on his games."

He looked at me dull-eyed, did not move.

"Why were you backing Tommy, Titanic?"

For nearly a full minute, he just stared at me. Then he stirred a little. "I owed him something. When I was in Reno a year ago, some of the local boys decided my straight play was ruining their jobbing. They sent a couple of torpedoes. They caught me with my pants down. Tommy Content had wind of it and came along and shot me out of the hole."

"And?"

"Later on, he went broke out there and wrote me he'd like to try New York. So I brought him on."

"And set him up with a bank account which you guaranteed."

His eyes got ever so much narrower, but he said nothing.

I prodded: "And then you find out about this Mary D'Estelle, better known as Dixie Higgins."

"Yeah," he admitted after another minute. "I found out about her."

"Mind telling me how?"

It took him an interminable time to make up his mind on that one. "I guess not," he said finally. "I was in Tommy's apartment yesterday afternoon. She called and left a message for him to call her. She said she had some information to sell about how somebody was gypping somebody."

"Yes, she did," I sneered.

His face was as immobile as a pillow. "All right," he said softly. "*You* tell *me*."

"Sure, I'll tell you. Tommy Content met up with Dixie. You know what she is—larceny from her head to her waist and from her knees to her toes. She—or she and Tommy—started playing ducks and drakes with your money—that is, the bank account you stood behind. I don't know yet what they were doing with it, but they lost plenty."

"Wait a minute," he stopped me softly. "I'm very interested in all this, but did you say Tommy has been *losing?*"

"Don't kid me," I growled. "You know as well as I do that that bank account is plenty in the red."

WE LOCKED EYES for seconds. "No," he said at last. "As it happens, it isn't. I stood beside Tommy when he called the bank and got the balance day before yesterday. He had put together about thirty odd thousand."

"You heard the bank tell him that?"

"Well, no. But I heard him ask and saw him write it down."

I made a weary gesture. "This isn't getting us anywhere—this dodging and slipping. You know damned well that they've dropped plenty—just how, I don't know. But the fact that he didn't mention the girl to you—or did he?"

"No, he didn't. That's why I got curious after he was killed and went down there—I remembered her phone number—and took a look for her."

"You tell a good story," I admired. "But you're getting in deep water now. I like it better this way: Dixie called and was lucky enough to stumble on you. Like the little tart she is, she bargained with you."

"Bargained with me? How?"

"She and Tommy had made their play with the bank account—and flopped. The end of the month is just a couple of days away, when the whole thing would break—to you. She figured to chisel get-away money, at least, from you before springing—and I can't imagine you refusing to pay—at *any* time—for information that you were being gypped. Or maybe she figured to beg off for herself by squealing.

"So you came down and—one way or another—she was shifty enough to blow the whistle on Tommy without you jumping her. So you went and waited up for Tommy and paid him off. Then, today, you got to thinking that she might squeal on the whole business and put you in a spot, so you started after her, ran her down—and here we are."

Not so much as a flicker of expression was in his eyes or face as he stared at me, and through me. Finally he said: "You must be crazy."

"No," I said. "I'm not crazy. Take off—"

There was sudden quick tapping at the door. I did not turn, just tightened my grip on the gun. To the heavily-breathing banker behind me I said: "Ask who it is."

His stammering voice was like a frog's croak as he choked out: "Who—who is it?"

Al Hackett's voice said: "Western Union."

"All right. Open it," I told Brandt.

I swung around so as to cover the whole room, as he unlatched the door with shaking hands. It *was* Al Hackett. He came in behind a gun, stopped, gasped at what he saw, then said hurriedly: "I'll be damned! Ace—listen—I figured you'd be here so I came right along. The punk's gone."

"*What?*"

"He's not at the Marquis' apartment," he poured out breathlessly. "Look—he left this note."

"Read it to me," I told him.

He stuffed his gun in his pocket, crackled paper and read: "Dear Mr. McGuire—I got to thinking and it come to me that I ought to get out of town. So I am going. By getting out of town I will get away from the guys who are gunning for me and I have got enough dough to get a fresh start somewheres else. I guess you could take care of me O.K. but I ain't had very good luck in this town and all in all I will be glad to see the last of it and get somewheres where people respect a guy. You can tell anybody that wants to know that I won't be back. Yours respectfully, Joseph Davies.”

Hack finished reading it and then blurted: “It’s wrote on the Marquis’ typewriter, Ace. I’ll bet ten to one he didn’t write it—that somebody—”

“Relax,” I said. “He wrote it.”

I WAS TIGHT and calm and poised on my toes, when I told Titanic: “I get it now—all of it. Take off your coat—drop that nail brush and take off your coat and shirt.” And when he hesitated, I snarled: “I’m not fooling, Titanic. *Take them off!* Or I’ll shoot a leg off you and take them off.”

He might have been nodding vague agreement to a comment on the weather. He dropped the brush, slowly unbuttoned coat, vest and shirt. A minute later they were a heap on the bed at the dead woman’s feet.

He had a perfectly hairless but well-formed torso. Not till you saw it naked did you realize that there was not an ounce of fat on him. I said, “Turn around,” and he turned.

After I had looked him over for a minute, I said, “Raise your arms,” and he did that, and then: “Lower them and scrounge your arms outwards.”

“O.K.,” I said presently. “You didn’t kill the girl. Whoever killed the girl killed Tommy—and did his best for me and Mr. Brandt there. And whoever did this got scratched—that’s why her nails were being scrubbed—to get the killer’s blood and flesh out from under them. You’re clear. Put your clothes back on and pick up your gun.”

“No,” Lester Brandt’s suddenly shrill, trembling voice croaked frenziedly. “No! Stand where you are! Drop that gun, McGuire!”

Naturally, I didn't drop it. I had it across my chest—he couldn't see that, being half behind me—with the muzzle under my arm. To drop it would have been signing death warrants for the three of us. His only possible out was to wipe us all out. I hadn't exactly seen him inch, step by step, back till he was in the corner, flanking Al Hackett as well as me but I had known he was doing it, if you get what I mean.

I let off roaring hell in the room.

I shot him twice in the chest, nailed him to the wall. He got off one shot that plowed gruesomely into the dead woman on the bed, making the whole bed rock a little. Then his hands came tight up to his chest as though he were trying to pull it up to his chin and his face was twisted in a grimace of terrible pain. The gun clattered to the floor—and he crashed to knees, to face.

Hackett, completely floored, yammered shrilly. "My God, my God—he—"

"Certainly, he. Don't ask me why he turned wolf—maybe because he was brought up rich and couldn't stand being poor—or maybe because he got this Dixie Higgins for a mistress and she talked him round. Anyway, he started to—" I dived at the pain-contorted Lester Brandt as he pushed himself desperately up from the floor, started a hand for his fallen gun.

I kicked it into a corner and he just sat there, half-propped, let his head droop. He said in a blurting sob: "She—she talked me into it. I—I told her I had a tip—"

"A tip on what?"

"I—a radio man I knew—said war news coming—knock the bottom out of foreign exchange. I had no capital to play it—she tempted me—I just meant to borrow—"

"There spoke a man," I said contemptuously. "Well, whoever doped it out, the story's the same as I just told it about Tommy—except that *Brandt* was the one running the racket, putting forged checks through the account with his O.K. on them. And that it was Tommy he knocked off when his speculations on foreign exchange went sour.

"But he wasn't willing to let it go and take the rap. From the minute when Tommy called him and asked his balance, he knew he had to move. So he first knocked off Tommy, then set about getting the forged checks—which he had O.K.'d at the bank—out of the bank before the murder investigation got to them. The son-of-a-witch picked me for a fall guy, arranged it so that I'd carry the checks out of the place and so that he could arrange an accident—God knows where he got the guts to take a chance on that—and get the checks destroyed or made useless for forgery comparison.

"Once he could do that, he was in the clear—except for little Dixie here, who could still blow the whole racket. So—while he was supposed to be waiting for me at the bank—he must have slipped down here and fixed her up. Well, there it is—take it away. If we haven't raised enough hell here to bring cops, go and phone some—but before you do, phone the newspapers and get the story on the streets. I wouldn't want the Marquis to have to come back to a piece of business that wasn't all cleaned up."

HACK HAS A one-track mind sometimes. He stood there gawking, but he couldn't get past the one bug that had apparently lodged in his mind from the first. "You—you mean that, after all, that poker game was on the level? That Joe Davies *took*

Tommy Content and Pfluger and the Ottheimers? And that Titanic here didn't have anything to do with the whole racket?"

"No," I said, "I don't mean anything of the kind." I reached over and plucked the note from Hackett's feet where it had fallen in the excitement. Titanic's eyes were glowing, lambent.

"No," I repeated, "I don't mean any such thing. Titanic touched off the whole business."

"What?" his eyes jerked up, half-foggily. "I—what?"

"You touched off the whole business. When you finally got this brain wave day before yesterday you went to Tommy and asked him to handle it, didn't you?"

He nodded slowly.

"And Tommy called the bank to check his balance, eh? How much did you tell him to lose to Joe Davies?"

"Twenty."

"O.K. He called to see if he had that much there. And he got Brandt here on the phone. Brandt had to lie—had to give him the balance that he would have had if Brandt hadn't been milking the account. So he knew he had to go into action—fast, before the lie caught up to him."

"Wait a minute," Hackett almost sobbed. "What *is* this? Titanic sent Tommy to *lose* money to Joe Davies? But Ottheimer—Pfluger—"

"Take a look at these glasses." I tossed them to him from my pocket. "They're spotters. Tommy rang in cards that had marks on the back—marks that were only visible through those glasses. What he won from the others, he lost to Joe."

"It isn't possible!" Hackett wailed. "He ran a crooked game—to *lose*? Why? In God's name, why?"

"After seeing Joe Davies react to a wad of money you're

asking that? You dope, you're gazing at Titanic Johnson's latest scheme to get rid of Joe Davies—as nice a bit of psychological figuring as I've ever seen. Having tried every other known way of prying him loose from Naomi, he finally got the combination—little friend Joe can't stand prosperity."

I looked at my watch. It was twenty to twelve. I threw the note carelessly on the bed and turned over toward the now unconscious killer. Over my shoulder I said: "You can have the note, Titanic. And you'd better get going. You wouldn't want to miss that floor show tonight of all nights, would you?"

The sound he made in his throat nobody could understand. He went out quickly.